Sara Sigourney Rice

Edgar Allan Poe

A memorial volume

Sara Sigourney Rice

Edgar Allan Poe
A memorial volume

ISBN/EAN: 9783337132149

Printed in Europe, USA, Canada, Australia, Japan

Cover: Foto ©Raphael Reischuk / pixelio.de

More available books at **www.hansebooks.com**

EDGAR ALLAN POE.

A Memorial Volume

BY

SARA SIGOURNEY RICE.

BALTIMORE:
TURNBULL BROTHERS.
1877.

Innes & Company, *Printers.*   F. H. Lucas, *Electrotyper.*

Contents.

ILLUSTRATIONS.

PREFACE.

So general an interest has been shown in the erection of the monument to

EDGAR ALLAN POE,

that it has been thought that a small volume as a memorial of the occasion would not be unacceptable to admirers of that poet.

It is perhaps not altogether a coincidence that almost at the same time that the poet's last resting-place was marked by the marble that commemorates his genius, his good name was also cleared from the calumnies that had darkened it for a generation. In his case justice was slow in coming, but it came at last; and no one who feels the power of Poe's rare, ethereal and pure genius, or is touched by his sad fate, need now grieve to think that his grave is unnoted or his reputation darkened.

To assist in commemorating this double justice, is the object of this volume.

Thanks are due to the various friends who have helped in the work: to Mr. J. H. INGRAM of London (to whose patient labor the world is chiefly indebted for the vindication of the poet's memory), who modified and adapted for this volume the biogra-

phical sketch prepared by him for the *International Review*; to
Col. J. T. L. PRESTON, of Lexington, Virginia, for the interesting
reminiscences of Poe's school-boy life; to the distinguished poets
whose tributes to his memory adorn our pages; to Mr. GEORGE
W. CHILDS of Philadelphia for generous assistance; to Mr. JOHN
T. MORRIS of Baltimore for valuable help and encouragement
from first to last; to Dr. WM. HAND BROWNE of Baltimore for
literary aid in the preparation of the work; to Mr. THOMAS H.
DAVIDSON of Abingdon, Virginia, for permission to copy the
unequalled portrait of Poe in his possession; and to all others
who have given words of approval and encouragement.

S. S. R.

BALTIMORE, *November*, 1876.

The annexed certificate from the well-known photographer, Mr.
Daniel Bendann, confirms the claim we have made for the likeness
of Poe which forms our frontispiece.

"BALTIMORE, *Nov.* 10, 1875.

The photograph of Edgar Allan Poe accompanying this volume
is from the original daguerreotype taken at the old Whitehurst
Gallery, Main St., Richmond, (with which establishment I was
myself for some time connected), and is, unquestionably, the most
faithful likeness of him extant.

DANIEL BENDANN."

EDGAR ALLAN POE.

A Biographical Sketch.

HERO-WORSHIP is as rampant in the United States as in any other of the so-called civilised countries; and even the Chinese custom of ennobling the ancestors, dead and buried though they may be, of a man who has done anything notable, is not unknown to the Americans. It is not strange, therefore, to learn that a gentle lineage has been found for Edgar Allan Poe, and that the daring deeds and reckless bravery of his ancestry

1

have been unearthed and re-chronicled, to prove that his virtues and vices came by right of birth. "Good wine needs no bush," and a man needs no coat-of-arms to ratify his right of entering the Temple of Fame. For our part, we are contented to begin Edgar Poe's story with his birth, which occurred at Boston on the 19th of January, 1809. In 1815 his youthful parents both died within a few weeks of each other, of consumption, leaving Edgar and two other children utterly destitute. Although only six years old at this time, the boy is stated to have been already noted for his precocity and beauty, and would seem to have gained the admiration, if he did not win the affection, of his godfather, Mr. Allan, a wealthy and intimate acquaintance of his deceased parents. Mr. Allan adopted him; and although little that is authentic can be learned of his early days, it may be worth record that a tenacious memory and a musical ear are said to have enabled him to learn by rote, and declaim with great effect, the finest passages of English poetry to the evening visitors at his godfather's house. Scarcely, however, had the little orphan time to get accustomed to his new home, when he was taken away to Europe by the Allans, and in his seventh year left at a school in Stoke Newington, then a distinct town, but now a portion of London. Poe seems to have looked back upon his sojourn in England with anything but ungrateful reminiscences. That he declared the description of the school and school-life in his tale of "William Wilson" a faithful reproduction of his own residence in the Stoke Newington Manor House School, is probably correct; while much, doubtless, of the gloom and glamor of his writings had their origin in the strangeness and friendlessness he must have experienced during his stay in that foreign and "excessively ancient house." The dreamy walks and mouldering dwellings that abounded in the neighborhood, could not fail to exert a strong influence upon a mind so morbidly sensitive as Poe's; nor can it be doubted that at the same time, in the *lustrum* of his life spent in England, he acquired a portion of that curious and *outré* classic lore which in after-years became one of the chief ornaments of his weird and wonderful works.

In 1821 the lad was recalled to America, and placed by his adopted father at an academy in Richmond, Virginia. Mr. Allan seems to have been really proud of his handsome and precocious godson, and to have indulged him in all that money could purchase; but neither alternate pettings and punishings, nor the state of domestic affairs at home, were well adapted to draw out the proud, yet affectionate, boy's better feelings. Through life Poe was sensitively acute to kindness; and when he was, or *believed* himself repulsed by human beings, his intense longing for sympathy drove him to seek for companionship in the society of dumb creatures. "There is something in the unselfish and self-sacrificing love of a brute," he remarked, "which goes directly to the heart of him who has had frequent occasion to test the paltry friendship and gossamer fidelity of mere *man*." In the best and most consistent work on Poe which has yet appeared,* a very characteristic and well verified anecdote is related of him, referring to the time when he was a student in the Richmond Academy. While it strikingly illustrates his tenderness of feeling and the constancy of his attachments, it but too clearly demonstrates how little affection or sympathy the young orphan found at his adopted home.

"He one day," says Mrs. Whitman, "accompanied a schoolmate to his home, where he saw for the first time Mrs. Helen S——, the mother of his young friend. This lady on entering the room took his hand and spoke some gentle and gracious words of welcome, which so penetrated the sensitive heart of the orphan boy as to deprive him of the power of speech, and for a time almost of consciousness itself. He returned home in a dream, with but one thought, one hope in life — to hear again the sweet and gracious words that had made the desolate world so beautiful to him, and filled his lonely heart with the oppression of a new joy. This lady afterward became the confidante of all his boyish sorrows, and hers was the one redeeming influence that saved and guided him in the earlier days of his turbulent and passionate youth."

* "Edgar Poe and his Critics." By S. H. Whitman.

Haplessly for the poor lad, the lady was herself overwhelmed with fearful and peculiar sorrows, and at the time when her guiding voice was most needed, died. But her poor boyish admirer could not endure the thought of her lying lonely and forsaken in the chilly grave, and for months after her decease he would nightly visit the neighboring cemetery in which she was entombed, to sob out his sorrow over the last resting-place of his first and never forgotten friend. When the nights were very dreary and cold, when the autumnal rains fell and the winds wailed mournfully over the graves, he lingered longer and came away most regretfully.

For many years, if not for life, the memory of this unfortunate lady tinged all his fancies and filled his mind with melancholy things. Within a twelvemonth of his death, writing to a friend, the truest friend, in all probability, of his "lonesome latter years," Poe broke through his usual reticence as to his early life, and confessed that his exquisite stanzas beginning, "Helen, thy beauty is to me," were inspired by the memory of this lady —"the one idolatrous and purely ideal love" of his tempest-tossed boyhood. In the early versions of his juvenile poems the name of Helen frequently recurs, and it was undoubtedly to this lady that he inscribed "The Pæan," a boyish piece, which he subsequently greatly improved both in rhythm and expression, and republished under the musical name of Lenore. In this little-known incident of Poe's life, Mrs. Whitman is undoubtedly justified in believing may be found "a key to much that seems strange and abnormal in the poet's after-life." In those solitary churchyard vigils, with all their associated memories, should doubtless be sought the clew to the psychological phenomena of Poe's strange existence; and that mind, as he himself remarked, which should strive to reduce his "phantasm to the common-place," must know and even study this phase of his being. The imagination which could so stead-fastly trace, step by step, the terrible stages of *sentience in death*, as Edgar Poe's does in his weird "Colloquy of Monos and Una,"

must indeed have been that of one who had oft and o'er sought to
wrest its earthy secrets from the charnel-house.

Returning to the more common-place records of the future poet's
story, he is found described at this period of his life, as remarkable
for general ability and feats of activity, for his wayward temper,
extreme personal beauty, power of extemporaneous tale-telling, and
his precocious knowledge of languages, mathematics, and different
branches of the natural sciences. Truly a long list of accomplishments, and one that if not vouched for by something more substan-
tial than the *ipse dixit* of an admirer, might well be discredited.
Thoroughly well-grounded, apparently, in these various studies, he
was sent by his adopted father to the University of Virginia, at
Charlottesville, in further pursuit of learning. Poe signed the
matriculation book of the Institution, on the 14th of February,
1826, and remained in good standing until the termination of the
session in the following December. Short as was his university
career, he left sufficient traces behind him to make *alma mater* not
only able but willing to refute the aspersions cast upon her distinguished child by Griswold and his followers.

"He entered the schools of Ancient and Modern Languages," says his classmate, Mr. Wertenbaker, now Secretary to the Faculty, "attending the lectures
on Latin, Greek, French, Spanish, and Italian. I was myself a member of the
last three classes, and can testify that he was tolerably regular in his attendence,
and a successful student, having obtained distinction at the Final Examina-
tions in Latin and French; and this was at that time the highest honor a
student could obtain, the present regulations in regard to degrees having not
then been adopted. Under existing regulations he would have graduated in
the two languages above named, and have been entitled to diplomas."

From the same official source we learn that Prof. Blatteman
having, on one occasion, desired his Italian class to render a portion
of Tasso's poem into English verse, not as a class exercise, but as
a beneficial method of study, Poe was the only student who responded to the suggestion, and for his performance was highly

complimented by the Professor. Such conduct, it is not surprising to learn, obtained him a good reputation among the Professors, while his uniformly sober, quiet, and orderly demeanor gained him an equally favorable character among the officers of the university; the records of which "attest that at no time during the session did he fall under the censure of the Faculty." It will sound strange to those who did not know him, to find that not only was Poe liked by the governing powers, but also that he was a great favorite among his classmates. Besides his naturally pleasing manner, he was great at athletic feats, a thing which always gains the admiration of young men, especially of students. One of his deeds of hardihood, and one which, if not proved by good authority, might have been relegated to the depths of that limbo where so many of the wonders told of Poe should be consigned, was the swimming from Ludlam's wharf to Warwick, on the James River, a distance of six miles, against a strong tide. When the truth of this story was questioned, Poe, who hated contradiction, obtained a certificate of the fact from several witnesses. This document declared, moreover, that "Mr. Poe did not seem at all fatigued, and walked back to Richmond immediately after the feat, which was undertaken for a wager." Such confidence had the poet, indeed, in his swimming powers, that he asserted his belief that on a favorable day he could swim across the English Channel, from Dover to Calais. In addition to all these occupations, he is stated to have attended debating societies, taken long rambles in the Blue Ridge mountains, and, as he was a clever draughtsman, to have had the habit of covering the walls of his dormitory with rough charcoal sketches. A very interesting and suggestive memento of his residence at Charlottesville is a copy from the register, of a list of books which Poe borrowed from the library while he was a student: Rollin's "Histoire Ancienne," "Histoire Romaine," Robertson's "America," Marshall's "Washington," Voltaire's "Histoire Particulière," and Dufief's "Nature Displayed." Those who have studied his works know what good use he made of this selection.

But this wonderful catalogue of accomplishments must not be accepted as entirely without alloy. Poe was not superhuman in his virtues. His morbid sensibility and proud self-reliance, both separately and conjointly, often led him into mischief. It has been told that his venturesome swimming feat was undertaken for a wager: in that he was successful; but success could not always attend his deeds of daring. A love of cards led him into extravagance, and he himself is averred, in conversation with a classmate, to have regretted his waste of money, confessing to a total indebtedness of $2000; certainly no very large sum for the heir of a wealthy man, but enough, apparently, to excite the anger of his adopted father, if unproved statements may be accepted as facts. Poe returned home; but the following year, 1827, roused by the efforts the Greeks were making to emancipate themselves from the Turkish yoke; uncomfortable, undoubtedly, at home; and probably emulous of Byron, whose example had excited the chivalric boys of both continents, he and an acquaintance, Ebenezer Berling, determined to start for Greece and offer their aid to the insurgents. Why, is not stated, but Mr. Berling did not go, while the embryo poet did; at least so it is declared, although what became of him—where he went and what his adventures were—is still unknown. Poe seems to have been very reticent upon the subject of his year's absence, and to have left uncontradicted the various stories invented, and even published during his life-time, to account for the interregnum in his history. The legend of his having gone to St. Petersburg and got involved in difficulties that necessitated ministerial aid for his extrication, must be abandoned, as must also the suggestion made by the anonymous author of a scurrilous paper, that Poe came to London and formed the acquaintance of Leigh Hunt and Theodore Hook, and lived "as that class of men—dragging out a precarious existence in garrets, doing drudgery work, writing for the great presses and for the reviews, whose world-wide celebrity has been the fruit of such men's labor." The ignorance displayed by these words of English men and letters, needs no comment.

Poe does not reappear upon the scene until the beginning of March, 1829, reaching Richmond, Virginia, too late to take a last farewell of his adopted mother, she having been interred the very day before his return home. Mrs. Allan seems to have exercised a conciliatory power in the household, where, it is said, it was frequently needed; and the poor lad, who in after-life invariably spoke well of this lady, doubtless soon felt the effects of her loss. Mr. Allan does not appear to have received his adopted son very cordially; but when Poe expressed his willingness to devote himself to the military profession, he exerted his influence and obtained a nomination to a scholarship in the West Point Military Academy. As each cadet at this institution was allowed twenty-eight dollars monthly, the poet, for such he now was, was, to some extent, rendered independent of his godfather's support. Poe's first generally known essay in literature, a little volume of poems, entitled "Al Aaraaf, Tamerlane, and Minor Poems," was published this year in Baltimore. An earlier volume of verse, entitled "Tamerlane and Other Poems," had been published in Boston in 1827, but was suppressed through circumstances of a private nature, and copies of it are exceedingly rare. The West Point records prove that Poe was admitted as a cadet on the 1st of July, 1830. He is declared to have entered upon his new mode of living with customary energy, but speedily discovered how totally unsuited to him now were the strict discipline and monotonous training of the Military Academy. The wayward and erratic course of existence to which he had long been accustomed, together with the fact of his having been so long a time sole master of his own actions, rendered it impossible for him to submit to the galling restraints of this institution. A fellow cadet with him at the Academy speaks of "his utter inefficiency and state of abstractedness at that place. He could not, or would not," he remarks, "follow its mathematical requirements. His mind was off from the matter-of-fact routine of the drill, which, in such a case as his, seemed practical joking, on some ethereal, visionary expedition. He was marked," adds the writer, "for an early grave." The place, indeed, was utterly unsuited to one of Poe's age, temperament and experience; it was but another edition of Pegasus at the plough, and the climax was, as would not have been difficult to foresee, that on the 7th of January, 1831, he was tried by a general court-martial "for various neglects of duty and disobedience of orders," which, however, consisted solely in absence from various drills. He was found guilty, and on the subsequent 6th of March was dismissed the service of the United States.

While still a cadet, and all unawed by the impending sentence, he published an enlarged edition of his boyish rhymes, as "Poems by Edgar A. Poe." This volume was for private circulation, and was dedicated to "The United States Corps of Cadets." This dedication appears to have drawn upon its unfortunate author the ridicule of his fellow-cadets, and one of them, alluding to the contents of the little volume, says: "These verses were the source of great merriment with us boys, who considered the author cracked, and the verses ridiculous doggerel." Happily for literature, the opinion of "us boys" did not carry much weight, and Poe continued to write "verses," all .egardless of West Point and its judgments. This little, forgotten book—it contained only 124 pages—is very interesting, not only on account of its cleverly written prefatory letter of seventeen pages, but also from the fact that it contains a large quantity of verse suppressed in subsequent editions of Poe's works. The omissions are as happy as have been the additions to these boyish poems, and notably mark the progress of their author's genius. No regard for the relics of his youth withheld Edgar A. Poe in after-life from pruning away the excrescences of his juvenile verse: with unswerving hand the critic clipped and molded his material into artistic unity.

Whatever may have been Mr. Allan's ideas as to the expulsion of his adopted son from the Military Academy, he received the prodigal, and apparently on the old footing. Poe had not been back long in Richmond before he became attached to a Miss Royster, and ultimately, it is believed, engaged to her. The lady's father seems to have been opposed to the match, and the engagement—if there was an engagement—was broken off. A violent quarrel took place between the old man and his godson, and the result was that they parted, never to meet again. Poe is stated to have now started off with the intention of proceeding to Poland to assist the Poles in their struggle against Russia, but does not appear to have left the American shores, probably restrained by the intelligence of the fall of Warsaw, an event which took place on the 6th of September, 1831. At this time, as if to complete the estrangement between the chivalric young poet and his godfather, Mr. Allan took unto himself a young wife, "the beautiful Miss Paterson," and, as if to give the death-blow to all hope, Miss Royster married Mr. Shelton, a man of fortune. Aimless and resourceless, Poe's position was indeed a sad one. Whither he went and what he did is a mystery not yet unravelled, but that he tried to support himself by literature is pretty evident. It is alleged that during the dreary interregnum of the next two years some of his finest tales were written · but, be that as it may, he had to prove that the waters of Helicon were anything but Pactolian. In 1833, the proprietor of the Baltimore "Saturday Visitor" offered money prizes for the best prose story and the best poem. Poe, who was in that city, selected and sent in six of his stories, under the title of "Tales of the Folio Club," and his poem of "The Coliseum." The well-known literary men who adjudicated upon this occasion, unanimously decided that the author of "The Folio Club" tales, who was of course unknown to them, was entitled to both the premiums. With his usual recklessness, Griswold writes the story of the award thus:

" Such matters are usually disposed of in a very off-hand way. Committees

to award literary prizes drink to the payer's health in good wines, over unex-
amined manuscripts, which they submit to the discretion of publishers, with
permission to use their names in such a way as to promote the publisher's
advantage. So, perhaps, it would have been in this case, but that one of the
committee, taking up a little book remarkably beautiful and distinct in calligraphy, was tempted to read several pages; and becoming interested, he
summoned the attention of the company to the half-dozen compositions it
contained. It was unanimously decided that the prizes should be paid to 'the
first of geniuses who had written legibly.' *Not another manuscript was unfolded.*
Immediately the 'confidential envelope' was opened, and the successful competitor was found to bear the *scarcely* known name of Poe."

A very slight examination of this story, apart from the direct
evidence obtained against it, might have convinced any impartial
reasoner that in this, as in most of his unremitting efforts to
underrate Poe's ability, Griswold has overshot the mark. It may
not have occurred to him that honorable men, with reputations to
maintain, could not be got to act in the way he describes; but his
own knowledge of publishing might have taught him that "the
publisher's advantage" would ·be promoted better by careful
examination of the submitted manuscripts than by leaving them
unfolded. That Poe's name was entirely unknown, and not
scarcely known to the adjudicators, need hardly be pointed out.
It is gratifying to know that not only was Griswold's assertion
emphatically denied by Messrs. Kennedy and Latrobe, the two
surviving adjudicators, but that the printed award itself contains
evidence contradicting it. "Among the prose articles were *many*
of various and distinguished merit," runs the statement, "but the
singular force and beauty of those sent by the author of ' The Tales
of the Folio Club,' leave us no room for hesitation in that department," etc., etc., which demonstrates two things: that there had
been some doubt in the poem department, and that Poe was
entirely unknown to the awarders of the prize. So much for the
value of Griswold's testimony, circumstantial as it seems.

Mr. Kennedy, the well-known author of "Horse-shoe Robin-

son" and other popular works, was so interested in the unknown
competitor that he invited him home, and Poe's response, written
in his usual clear and exquisite calligraphy, proves to what a
depth of misery he had sunk. "Your invitation to dinner has
wounded me to the quick," he pathetically declares. "I can not
come for reasons of the most humiliating nature — my personal
appearance. You may imagine my mortification in making this
disclosure to you, but it is necessary." Urged by the noblest
feelings, the popular author at once sought out the unfortunate
youth, and found him, as he declares, almost starving. Recog-
nising his worth, Mr. Kennedy at once became his friend, and it
is interesting to know that nothing was ever done by Poe to forfeit
this friendship, as indeed Mr. Kennedy, when informed of the
poet's decease, declared. It seems impossible to credit any of Griswold's stories of Poe's ungrateful behavior, when we find so many
persons testifying to his goodness of heart. Mr. Kennedy, so far
from contenting himself with mere courtesies, assisted his young
protégé to re-establish himself in the outward garb of respectability,
and treated him more like a dear relative than a chance acquaintance. In his diary of this date he records: "I gave him clothing,
free access to my table, and the use of a horse for exercise whenever
he chose; in fact, brought him up from the verge of despair."

During this era in his life, his godfather's second wife having
presented her husband with a son, Poe's prospects of inheritance
were destroyed; indeed, when Mr. Allan died, in the spring of
1834, all expectations of receiving any portion of his wealth were
put an end to by a will in which he was not mentioned. Assisted
by Mr. Kennedy and other literary men, however, by constant
drudgery he contrived to earn a livelihood. In August of this
year a Mr. White, an energetic and accomplished man, projected
the "Southern Literary Messenger." At the suggestion of Mr.
Kennedy, Poe sent some of his stories to the new magazine, and
in March 1835 Mr. White published, with some flattering com-

ments, " Berenice." Mr. Kennedy had now had eighteen months'
experience of Poe without finding anything to alter his opinion of
him, and in April wrote the following letter with reference to him
to Mr. White :—

"DEAR SIR — Poe did right in referring to me. He is very clever with his
pen—classical and scholarlike. He wants experience and direction, but I have
no doubt he can be made very useful to you. And, poor fellow ! he is *very*
poor. I told him to write something for every number of your magazine, and
that you might find it to your advantage to give him some permanent employ.
He has a volume of very bizarre tales in the hands of ———, in Philadelphia,
who for a year past has been promising to publish them. This young fellow
is highly imaginative, and a little given to the terrific. He is at work on a
tragedy, but I have turned him to drudging upon whatever may make money,
and I have no doubt you and he will find your account in each other."

Mr. White did, undoubtedly, find his " account " in his new con-
tributor; and after the publication in the June number of the
"Messenger," of "Hans Pfaall,"—three weeks previous to the
appearance in the "New York Sun" of Mr. Locke's famous "Moon
Hoax," be it noted—found Poe's reputation increasing so rapidly,
that he was only too glad to act upon Mr. Kennedy's suggestion
of permanent employment, and offered to engage him to assist in
the editorial duties of his magazine at a salary of five hundred and
twenty dollars per annum. The young author willingly accepted
the appointment, and removed, in September 1835, from Baltimore
to Richmond, Virginia, where the "Messenger" was published.
The following letter, written to his friend Kennedy, to acquaint
him with the fact of his appointment, affords a sad picture of the
terrible melancholia under which the poet then, and so frequently,
suffered. This affliction, with which all who would know Poe
thoroughly should be acquainted, was not merely the result of pri-
vation and grief, but undoubtedly to some extent hereditary.

"RICHMOND, September 11, 1835.
"DEAR SIR — I received a letter from Dr. Miller, in which he tells me you

are in town. I hasten, then, to write you, and express by letter what I have always found it impossible to express orally — my deep sense of gratitude for your frequent and ineffectual assistance and kindness. Through your influence Mr. White has been induced to employ me in assisting him with the editorial duties of his magazine, at a salary of five hundred and twenty dollars per annum. The situation is agreeable to me for many reasons; but, alas! it appears to me that nothing can give me pleasure or the slightest gratification. Excuse me, my dear sir, if in this letter you find much incoherency. My feelings at this moment are pitiable indeed. I am suffering under a depression of spirits, such as I have never felt before. I have struggled in vain against the influence of this melancholy; *you will believe me*, when I say that I am still miserable, in spite of the great improvement in my circumstances. I say you will believe me, and for this simple reason, that a man who is writing for *effect* does not write thus. My heart is open before you; if it be worth reading, read it. I am wretched and know not why. Console me—for you can. But let it be quickly, or it will be too late. Write me immediately; convince me that it is worth one's while — that it is at all necessary to live, and you will prove yourself indeed my friend. Persuade me to do what is right. I do mean this. I do not mean that you should consider what I now write you a jest. Oh! pity me! for I feel that my words are incoherent; but I will recover myself. You will not fail to see that I am suffering under a depression of spirits which will ruin me should it be long-continued. Write me then, and quickly; urge me to do what is right. Your words will have more weight with me than the words of others, for you were my friend when no one else was. Fail not, as you value your peace of mind hereafter. E. A. Poe."

To this saddening wail of despair, Mr. Kennedy responded —

"I am sorry to see you in such plight as your letter shows you in. It is strange that just at this time, when everybody is praising you, and when fortune is beginning to smile upon your hitherto wretched circumstances, you should be invaded by these blue-devils. It belongs, however, to your age and temper to be thus buffeted — but be assured, it only wants a little resolution to master the adversary forever. You will doubtless do well henceforth in literature, and add to your *comforts*, as well as your reputation, which it gives me great pleasure to assure you is everywhere rising in popular esteem."

"These blue-devils" notwithstanding, the new editor worked wonders with the "Messenger." "His talents made that periodical quite brilliant, while he was connected with it," records Mr. Kennedy, and, indeed, in a little more than a twelvemouth, Poe

raised its circulation from seven hundred to nearly five thousand.
This success was partially due to the originality and fascination of
Poe's stories, and partially owing to the fearlessness of his trenchant
critiques. He could not be made, either by flattery or abuse, a
respecter of persons. In the December number of the "Messenger" he began that system of literary scarification—that crucial
dissection of bookmaking mediocrities, which, while it created
throughout the length and breadth of the States a terror of his
powerful pen, at the same time raised up against him a host of,
although *unknown*, implacable enemies, who, hereafter, were only
too glad to seize upon and repeat any story—never mind how
improbable—to his discredit. Far better would it have been for
his future welfare, if, instead of affording contemporary nonentities
a chance of literary immortality, by impaling them upon his pen's
sharp point, he had devoted his whole time to the production of
his wonderful stories, or still more wonderful poems. Why could
he not have left the task of crushing the works of his Liliputian
contemporaries to the ordinary "disappointed authors"?

During 1836, Poe devoted the whole of his time to the "Messenger," producing tales, poems, and reviews, in profusion; indeed,
at Mr. White's suggestion, apparently, frittering away his genius
over these latter. Early in the year, a gleam of hope seemed to
break in upon his hapless career. In Richmond, where he was
among his own kindred, he met, loved, and married his cousin
Virginia, the daughter of his father's sister. Miss Clemm was but
a girl in years, and was not unsuspected of inheriting symptoms
of the family complaint, consumption; but, undeterred by this, or
by his slender income, the poor poet was married to his kinswoman,
and, it must be confessed, in happier circumstances, a better or
more suitable helpmate could scarcely have been found for him,
while marriage had the further advantage of bringing him under
the motherly care of his aunt, Mrs. Clemm. In January 1837,
Poe resigned the editorial management of the "Southern Literary

Messenger," to accept the more lucrative employment offered him in New York. Mr. White parted from Poe very reluctantly, and in the number of the "Messenger" containing the announcement of his resignation, issued a note to the subscribers, wherein, after alluding to the ability with which the retiring editor had conducted the magazine, he remarked, "Mr. Poe, however, will continue to furnish its columns from time to time, with the effusions of his vigorous and popular pen." This incident is mentioned, and attention drawn to the fact, more than once acknowledged by Mr. White, that Poe *resigned for other employment*, because Griswold declares that he was dismissed for drunkenness.

From Richmond, Poe removed to New York, where he and his household took up their residence in Carmine street. Mr. Powell says, that in his writing for the "New York Quarterly Review," the poet "came down pretty freely with his critical axe, and made many enemies." An interesting sketch of Poe's *ménage* at this period of his history has been left us by the late Mr. William Gowans, the wealthy and respected, but eccentric New York bibliopolist. Alluding to the untruthfulness of the prevalent idea of Poe's character, the shrewd old man remarks :

"I therefore, will also show you my opinion of this gifted but unfortunate genius. It may be estimated as worth little, but it has this merit—it comes from an eye and ear witness; and this, it must be remembered, is the very highest of legal evidence. For eight months or more, one house contained us, us one table fed! During that time I saw much of him, and had an opportunity of conversing with him often, and I must say that I never saw him the least affected with liquor, nor even descend to any known vice, while he was one of the most courteous, gentlemanly, and intelligent companions I have met with during my journeyings and haltings through divers divisions of the globe; besides, he had an extra inducement to be a good man, as well as a good husband, for he had a wife of matchless beauty and loveliness, her eyes could match those of any houri, and her face defy the genius of a Canova to imitate; a temper and disposition of surpassing sweetness; besides, she seemed as much devoted to him and his every interest as a young mother is to her first-born. . . . Poe had a remarkably pleasing and prepossessing countenance ; what the ladies would call decidedly handsome."

In addition to this testimony, Mr. Gowans, in conversation with
Mr. Thomas C. Latto of New York, stated that he was a boarder
in the house of Mrs. Clemm, and that Poe and his young wife,
who was described as fragile in constitution, also boarded in the
same building.

"He only left when the household was broken up. Of course Mr. Gowans
had the best opportunity of seeing what kind of life the poet led. His testimony
is that he (Poe) was uniformly quiet, reticent, gentlemanly in demeanor, and
during the whole period he lived there, not the slightest trace of intoxication
or dissipation was discernible in the illustrious inmate, who was at that time
engaged in the composition of 'Arthur Gordon Pym.' Poe kept good hours,
and all his little wants were seen to both by Mrs. Clemm and her daughter,
who watched him as studiously as if he had been a child. Mr. Gowans,"
remarks Mr. Latto, "is himself a man of intelligence, and, being a Scotchman,
is by no means averse to 'a two-handed crack,' but he felt himself kept at a
distance somewhat, by Poe's aristocratic reserve."

During January and February of this year (1837), Poe contributed the first portions of "The Narrative of Arthur Gordon
Pym," to the "Messenger," and encouraged by the interest it
excited, he determined to complete it. It was not published in book
form, however, until July of the following year. Griswold declares
that it "received little attention" in America, and adds, copies of the
work being sent to England, "and it being mistaken at first for a
narrative of real experiences, it was advertised to be reprinted; but
a discovery of its character, *I believe*, prevented such a result."
The fact is, that in a short interval the story was several times
reprinted in England, and did attract considerable notice; the "air
of truth" which Griswold suggested was only in the attempt,
having excited much interest.

In the fall of 1838 Poe removed to Philadelphia, and entered
into an arrangement to write for the "Gentleman's Magazine" of
that city. His talents soon produced brilliant effects upon this
publication, and in May, 1839, he was appointed to the editorial
management, "devoting to it," says Griswold, "for ten dollars a

week, two hours every day, which left him abundant time for more important labors." What leisure his editorial duties may have left is unknown, but he certainly contrived to write for some other publications, and as several of his finest stories and most pungent critiques first made their appearance at this time, it is to be presumed that he contrived to earn a fair livelihood. In the fall of 1839 he made a collection of his best stories, and published them in two volumes as "Tales of the Grotesque and the Arabesque." This collection contained some of his most imaginative writings, and greatly increased his reputation. It included "The Fall of the House of Usher," a story containing his characteristic poem of "The Haunted Palace." Griswold avers that Poe was indebted to Longfellow's "Beleaguered City" for the idea of this exquisite poem, but that Poe asserted Longfellow owed the idea to him. As a rule, plagiarism is a charge easy to make, but hard to prove; and as some, if not all, of the letters ascribed by Griswold to Poe are evidently fabrications, his evidence will go for very little. It may, however, be pointed out that Poe's poem had been published long before Longfellow's, and not "a few weeks," as stated by Griswold, and in two different publications. The resemblance was probably accidental, but at all events Tennyson had worked out the same idea in "The Deserted House," published in 1830. In the same collection appeared Poe's favorite tale of "Ligeia." On a copy of this weird story, in my possession, is an indorsement by the poet to the effect that "Ligeia was also suggested by a *dream*"— the "also" referring to a poem sent to Mrs. Whitman, and which, he wrote to her, "contained all the events of a *dream*."

Notwithstanding the reputation which his tales brought him, he was frequently forced, by the *res angusta domi*, to forsake his legitimate province in literature, and turn his pen to any project that proffered a certain remuneration. There is a story told of him by Griswold, on the authority, he asserts, of a Philadelphia paper, to support his denunciation of Poe as a wholesale plagiarist. Poe, so runs the legend, reprinted a popular work on Conchology, written by the well-known naturalist, Captain Thomas Brown, as by himself, "and actually took out a copyright for the American edition of Captain Brown's work, and, omitting all mention of the English original, pretended in the preface to have been under great obligations to several scientific gentlemen of this city." For ten years after Poe's death this utterly improbable story circulated wherever the poet's biography was told; and although many persons must have known its untruth, no one ventured to explain the facts, till ultimately it came under the notice of Prof. Wyatt, the person of all others best able to disprove the tale, which he did through the "Home Journal." A man of considerable erudition and scientific attainments, Prof. Wyatt was publishing a series of works on Natural History, and among them was a "Manual of Conchology"; to this Poe, whose scientific knowledge was most comprehensive and exact, contributed so largely that the publisher was fully justified in putting his popular name on the title-page, although he only received a share of the profits. As both Brown's "Text Book" and Poe's "Manual" are founded on the system laid down by Lamarck, they necessarily resemble each other; but the absurd charge that one is plagiarised from the other, can only have arisen from gross ignorance or falsehood. About this same time Poe also published, as a sequence to such studies, a translation and digest of Lemmounier's "Natural History," and other works of a similar character.

Toward the close of 1840, Mr. George R. Graham, owner of the "Casket," acquired possession of the "Gentleman's Magazine," and merging the two publications, began a new series as "Graham's Magazine." Mr. Graham was only too willing to retain the services of the brilliant editor, and he found his reward in so doing. Edgar Poe, assisted by the proprietor's liberality to his contributors, in little more than two years raised the number of subscribers to the magazine from five to fifty-two thousand. His daring critiques, his analytic essays, and his weird stories, following one another in rapid succession, startled the public into a knowledge of his power. He created new enemies, however, by the dauntless intrepidity with which he assailed the fragile reputations of the small bookmakers, especially by the publication of his "Autography" papers. He also excited much criticism by the challenge contained in his papers on "Cryptography," wherein he promulgated the theory that human ingenuity could not construct any cryptograph which human ingenuity could not decipher. Tested by several correspondents with difficult samples of their skill, the poet actually took the trouble to examine and solve them, in triumphant proof of the truth of his proposition.

In April, 1841, appeared "The Murders in the Rue Morgue," the first of a series illustrating another analytic phase of Poe's many-sided mind. This story was the first to introduce his name to the French public, and, having caused a lawsuit not altogether conducive to a high estimate of the literary morality of France, gave an impetus to his reputation in that country, which culminated in the faithfully *vraisemblant* translations of Baudelaire, to whose efforts and genius are chiefly due the fact that Poe's tales have become standard classic works in the French language. Edgar Poe is, it should be pointed out, the only American writer really well known and popular in France; while in Spain his tales early acquired fame, and have now become thoroughly nationalised; they, with the exception of those on Spanish subjects by Irving, Prescott, and Motley, being the only American works known in that country. In Germany, Poe's poems and tales have been frequently translated; but owing to their characteristics having been mistaken, it is only quite recently that they have attained any widely diffused celebrity amongst the *native* Germans.

In 1842 appeared "The Descent into the Maelström," a tale that in many respects may be deemed one of his most marvellous and idiosyncratic. It is one of those tales which, like "The Gold Bug," demonstrates the untenability of the theory first promulgated by Griswold, and since so frequently echoed by his copyists, that Poe's ingenuity in unriddling a mystery was only ingenious in appearance, as he himself had woven the webs he so dexterously unweaves. The tales above cited, however, prove Griswold's systematic depreciation of Poe's genius. They are the secrets of nature which he unveils, and are not the riddles of art ; he did not invent the natural truth that a cylindrical body, swimming in a vortex, offered more resistance to its suction, and was drawn in with greater difficulty, than bodies of any other form of equal bulk, any more than he invented the mathematical ratio in which certain letters of the English language recur in all documents of any length. He did not invent "The Mystery of Marie Rogêt," but he tore away the mysteriousness and laid bare the truth in that strange story of real life. He did not invent, but he was the first to describe, if not to perceive, those peculiar idiosyncrasies of the human mind so wonderfully but so clearly portrayed in "The Murders in the Rue Morgue," "The Purloined Letter," "The Imp of the Perverse," and other wonderful examples of his mastery over the mental chords and wheels of our being.

It was during his brilliant editorship, it is believed, of "Graham's Magazine," that Poe discovered and first introduced to the American public the genius of Elizabeth Barrett Browning, and it was greatly due to him that her fame in America was coeval with, if it did not precede, that won by her in her native land. In May, 1841, he contributed to the Philadelphia "Saturday Evening Post"—a paper belonging to Mr. Graham—that *prospective* notice of the newly commenced story of "Barnaby Rudge," which drew from Dickens a letter of admiring acknowledgment. In this said notice the poet, with mathematical precision, explained and foretold the exact plot of the as yet unpublished story.

At the close of 1842, Poe resigned this post of joint editor and reviewer of "Graham's Magazine"; why or wherefore is not clearly known, but that it was not through drunkenness, as alleged by Griswold, his successor in the editorial duties, Mr. Graham's own testimony conclusively proves. Poe's cherished idea was to start a magazine of his own, but his resignation may perhaps be justly ascribed to that constitutional restlessness which from time to time overpowered him, and drove him from place to place in a vain search after the El Dorado of his hopes. The truth as to his severance from "Graham's," like so many of the details that enshroud and confuse his life's story, was probably purposely mystified by Poe, who had even a greater love than had Byron of mystifying the impertinent busybodies who wearied him for biographical information. It was shortly previous to this epoch in his life that he had the misfortune to make the acquaintance of Rufus Griswold, a man who, although several years Poe's junior in age, had by many years "knocking about the world," gained an experience of its shifts and subterfuges that made him far more than a match for the poet's unworldly nature. According to Griswold, his acquaintance with Poe began in the spring of 1841, by the poet calling at his hotel and leaving two letters of introduction, and he follows up his account of the interview with the quotation of several letters purporting to have been written by Poe. The enmity of Griswold for Poe—"the long, intense, and implacable enmity"—spoken of by John Neal and Mr. Graham, is so palpable to readers of the *soidisant* "Memoir," that it needed not the outside evidence which has been so abundantly furnished to prove it, and the wonder is, not so much that the biographer's audacious charges should have obtained credit abroad, but that no American should yet have produced so complete a refutation of them as could and *should* have been given years ago.

In the spring of 1843, the one hundred dollar prize offered by "The Dollar Newspaper," was obtained by Poe for his tale of "The Gold Bug," a tale illustrative of and originating in his theory of ciphers. As usual, Griswold, in alluding to it, can not refrain from displaying the cloven hoof, and knowing it to be the most popular of Poe's stories in America, refers to it "as one of the most remarkable illustrations of his ingenuity of construction and *apparent* subtlety of reasoning." In 1844 the poet removed to New York, whither his daily increasing fame had already preceded him. "For the first time," remarks Griswold, completely ignoring the talent of all other American cities, "for the first time he was received into circles capable of both the appreciation and the production of literature." It has generally been assumed that the first publication Poe wrote for in New York was the "Mirror," but the author of a sketch of Willis and his contemporaries, contributed to the Newark "Northern Monthly" in 1868, referring to Poe as

"One who has been more shamefully maligned and slandered than any other writer that can be named," remarks: "I say this from personal knowledge of Mr. Poe, who was associated with myself in the editorial conduct of my own paper *before* his introduction into the office of Messrs. Willis and Morris"; adding, "for Mr. Willis's manly vindication of the unfortunate, I honor him."

Again, referring to this vindication of Poe from Griswold's accusation, he says:

"Mr. Willis's testimony is freely confirmed by other publishers. On this subject I have some singular revelations which throw a strong light on the causes that darkened the life, and made most unhappy the death of one of the most remarkable of all our literary men, as an English reviewer once said, 'the most brilliant genius of his country.'"

In the fall of 1844, Poe was engaged as sub-editor and critic on the "Mirror," a daily paper belonging to N. P. Willis and General George Morris. Willis writing from Idlewild, in October 1859, to his fellow-poet and former partner, recalls to his memory that

"Poe came to us quite incidentally, neither of us having been personally acquainted with him till that time. . . . As he was a man who never smiled, and never said a propitiatory or deprecating word, we were not likely to have been seized with any sudden partiality or wayward caprice in his favor. . . . You remember how absolutely and how good-humoredly ready he was for any suggestion; how punctually and industriously reliable in the following out of the wish once expressed; how cheerful and present-minded at his work, when he might excusably have been so listless and abstracted."

During the whole six months or so that Poe was engaged on the "Mirror," Willis asserts that "he was invariably punctual and industrious," and was daily "at his desk from nine in the morning till the evening paper went to press." At this period some of the most remarkable productions of his genius, including his poetic *chef-d'œuvre* "The Raven," were given to the world. This unique and most original of poems first appeared in Colton's "American Review" for February, 1845, as by "Quarles." It was at once reprinted in the "Evening Mirror" with the author's name attached, and in a few weeks was known over the whole of the United States. It carried its author's name and fame from shore to shore; called into existence parodies and imitations innumerable; drew warm eulogies from some of the first of foreign poets, and finally made him the lion of the season. And for this masterpiece of genius—for this poem which has probably done more for the renown of American letters than any single work—it is alleged that Poe, then at the height of his renown, received the sum of ten dollars! Mrs. Browning, in a letter written soon after the republication of "The Raven" in England, says:

"This vivid writing—this *power which is felt*—has produced a sensation here in England. Some of my friends are taken by the fear of it, and some by the music. I hear of persons who are haunted by the 'Nevermore,' and an acquaintance of mine, who has the misfortune of possessing a bust of Pallas, can not bear to look at it in the twilight."

And then referring to Poe's "Mesmeric Revelations," which some journals accepted as a record of facts, the poetess resumes:

"Then there is a tale going the rounds of the newspapers about mesmerism, which is throwing us all into 'most admired disorder'—dreadful doubts as to whether it can be true, as the children say of ghost stories. The certain thing about it is the power of the writer."

The "Broadway Journal" was started by two journalists at the beginning of 1845, and in March, Poe was associated with them in its management. He had occasionally written for it from the first, but had nothing to do with the editorial arrangements until the tenth number. One of the most noticeable of his contributions was a critique on the poems of Elizabeth Barrett Browning, to whom he shortly afterwards dedicated, in most admiring terms, a selection of his poems, published by Messrs. Wiley & Putnam. In July of this year, the sole supervision of the "Broadway Journal" devolved upon Poe, but it was not until the following October that he became proprietor as well as editor of this publication. His predecessors do not appear to have invested much money or talent in the undertaking, and when they retired and left the poet in entire possession of the publication, its acquisition would not appear to have added much to his worldly goods. In March, he gave a lecture in the library of the New York Historical Society, on the American Poets, and attracted much attention, not only by the originality and courage of his remarks, but by the fascination of his presence, his eloquence, and his personal beauty. The *furor* which his lecture created caused him to be asked to Boston, and in the autumn he accepted an invitation to recite a poem in the Lyceum of that city.

"When he accepted the invitation," avers Griswold—who assumes to have known Poe's innermost thoughts—"he intended to write an original poem upon a subject which he said had haunted his imagination for years, but cares, anxieties, and feebleness of will prevented, and a week before the appointed night, he wrote to a friend imploring assistance. 'You compose with such astonishing facility,' he urged in his letter, 'that you can easily furnish one quite soon enough, a poem that shall be equal to my reputation.'. . . At last, instead of pleading illness, as he had previously done on a similar occasion, he determined to read his poem of 'Al Aaraaf.'"

It is difficult to say how much, if any, of this story is true; but as the lady died before the "Memoir" was published, Griswold, who was known to have been her confidant, was safe in telling the tale. One who was present on the occasion of the said recitation, states that the lecture course of the Boston Lyceum was waning in popularity, and that Poe's fame being at its zenith, he was invited to deliver a poem at the opening of the winter session.

"I remember him well," he remarks, "as he came on the platform. He was the best realisation of a poet in feature, air, and manner, that I have ever seen, and the unusual paleness of his face added to its aspect of melancholy interest. He delivered a poem that no one understood, but at its conclusion gave the audience a treat which almost redeemed their disappointment. This was the recitation of his own 'Raven,' which he repeated with thrilling effect. It was something well worth treasuring in memory. Poe," he adds, "after he returned to New York, was much incensed at Boston criticism on his poem."

The poet was not probably "incensed" to any very great extent, but doubtless found it a profitable hit for his journal to, as he styled it, "kick up a bobbery." A week after the lecture, therefore, he began to comment, in a tone of playful badinage, upon the remarks made with respect to it by the newspapers, especially the "Bostonian." Griswold reprinted nearly the whole of Poe's good-natured bantering in the "Memoir," and appears to have fancied something terrible was hidden in the jokes about the Bostonians and their "Frog Pond," and deems "it scarcely necessary to suggest that this must have been written before he had quite recovered from the long intoxication which maddened him at the time to which it refers." As "the time to which it refers" was evidently that of the lecture, and as it was written upward of a week after that event, and as Poe continued the discussion in the same tone three weeks later, as, indeed, the biographer notices, "the long intoxication" must, indeed, have been a "lengthy" one. Although these hurried newspaper jottings were, as Griswold himself admits, written when Poe was suffering from "cares, anxieties, and feebleness of will," and when, as he shows, the poor persecuted poet was in pecuniary difficulties, and, not being able to pay for assistance, was obliged somehow to write nearly all the "Journal" himself, yet, under all such conflicting ills, these few jocular, but overstrained jottings are unearthed and adduced as evidence of Poe's irretrievably bad nature.

During his possession of the "Broadway Journal," the labors of Edgar Poe must have been terrible : not only did his poverty compel him to contribute papers to other magazines, but week after week he wrote the larger portion of the "Journal's" folio pages himself, besides performing the many duties of an editorial proprietor. The "much friendly assistance," which Griswold—who said also that he was friendless—asserts he received in his management of the journal, being chiefly confined to the contribution of a few verses. He was only able to comply with this great strain upon his mental and physical strength by reprinting many of his published tales and poems in the columns of his paper, and even these were submitted to a close scrutiny, and innumerable alterations and corrections made in them. A journal of his own in which he could give vent to his own untrammelled opinions, unchecked by the mercantile and, undoubtedly, more prudential views of publishers, had long been one of Poe's most earnest desires, and he attained his wish in the possession of the "Broadway Journal "; but poverty, ill-health, want of worldly knowledge, and a sick, a dying wife, to distract him, all combined to overpower his efforts. What could the unfortunate poet do ? During the three months that he had complete control of the moribund journal, he made it, considering when it was published, and how, as good a cheap literary paper as was ever produced. All his efforts, however, were insufficient to keep it alive, so, on the 3d of January, 1846, he was obliged to resign his favorite hobby of a paper of his own. It may be pointed out that while in possession of the "Broadway," he availed himself of the opportunity of displaying his almost Quixotic feelings of gratitude toward those who had formerly befriended him, and not only to the living, whose aid might continue, but toward those who had already entered into the "hollow vale." His generous tributes to departed worth are truer proofs of his nobility of heart, than any disproof that malignity could invent.

In the winter of 1845-6, Edgar Poe was occasionally to be met with in the literary reunions of New York, and sometimes, says Mrs. Whitman, his fair young wife was seen with him. "She seldom took part in the conversation, but the memory of her sweet and girlish face, always animated and vivacious, repels the assertion, afterwards so cruelly and recklessly made, that she died a victim to the neglect and unkindness of her husband, who, it has been said, 'deliberately sought her death that he might embalm her memory in immortal dirges'." Gilfillan* declares that Poe caused the death of his wife that he might have a fitting theme for "The Raven"; but unfortunately for the truth of that gentleman's theory, the poem was published more than two years previous to the event he so ingeniously assumed it to commemorate. Friend and foe alike, who knew anything of Poe, bear testimony to the unvarying kindness and affection of the poet for his young wife. "His love for his wife," says Mr. Graham, "was a sort of rapturous worship. I have seen him hovering around her when she was ill, with all the fond fear and tender anxiety of a mother for her firstborn—her slightest cough causing in him a shudder, a heart-chill that was visible. . . It was this hourly *anticipation* of her loss that made him a sad and thoughtful man, and lent a mournful melody to his undying song." Mrs. Whitman remarks, that it was for his dear wife's sake, "and for the recovery of that peace which had been so fatally imperilled amid the irritations and anxieties of his New York life, that Poe left the city and removed to the little Dutch cottage in Fordham, where he passed the three remaining years of his life.'

---

* Mr. Gilfillan has since retracted this monstrous and absurd charge

In May, 1846, Poe began to contribute to "Godey's Lady's Book"
a series of critiques on the "Literati of New York." These essays
were immensely successful, but the caustic style of some of them
produced terrible commotion in the ranks of mediocrity, as may be
seen from Mr. Godey's notice to his readers respecting the anonymous and other letters he received concerning them. A Dunn-
English, or Dunn-Brown, for he is doubly named, dissatisfied with
the manner in which his literary shortcomings had been reviewed
by Poe, instead of waiting, as others did, for the poet's death, when
every ass could have its kick at the lion's carcass, "retaliated in a
personal newspaper article," remarks Duyckinck, in his invaluable
"Encyclopedia," "and the communication was reprinted in the
'Evening Mirror' in New York, whereupon Poe instituted a libel
suit against that journal, and recovered several hundred dollars."
Griswold's account of the affair is that "Dunn English chose to
evince his resentment of the critic's unfairness by the publication of
a card, in which he painted strongly the infirmities of Poe's life and
character." "Poe's article," he continues, "was entirely false in
what purported to be the facts," and, to support this audacious mis-
representation, he, in reprinting the said article, inserted a number
of personalities, *the whole of which are absent* from the real critique
published in the "Lady's Book"! It is thoroughly characteristic
of Griswold's utter recklessness that he declares Mr. Godey's refusal
to print Poe's rejoinder to English in the "Lady's Book," sent on
the 27th of June, led "to a disgraceful quarrel," and to the "prem-
ature conclusion" of the "Literati"; and that Poe "ceased to write
for the 'Lady's Book' in consequence of Mr. Godey's justifiable
refusal to print in that miscellany his 'Reply to Dr. English.'"
Poe's review of English appeared in the second or June number
of the "Literati," and when Griswold's habitual recklessness is
known, one is not surprised to find, upon reference to the magazine, that the sketches ran their stipulated course until the following
October, and that after that date, and until within a short time of

his decease, Poe continued to contribute to the "Lady's Book"; nor is one surprised to find Mr. Godey writing to the "Knickerbocker" in defence and praise of the poet's "honorable and blameless conduct." In January, 1847, the poet's darling wife died, and in an autographic letter now before us, Poe positively reiterates the accusation that she,—"My poor Virginia, was continually tortured (although not deceived) by anonymous letters, and on her deathbed declared that her life had been shortened by their writer," a writer whose infamy can only remain concealed through obscurity. The loss of his wife threw the poet into a melancholy stupor which lasted for several weeks; but nature reasserting her powers, he gradually resumed his wonted avocations. During the whole of the year Poe lived a quiet, secluded life with his mother-in-law, receiving occasional visits from his friends and admirers, and thinking out the great and crowning work of his life—"Eureka"—"that grand prose poem' to which he devoted the last and most matured energies of his wonderful intellect." Toward the close of this "most immemorial year," this year in which he had lost his cousin-bride, he wrote his weird monody of "Ulalume." Like so many of his poems it was autobiographical, and the poet declared it was in its basis, although not in the precise correspondence of time, simply historical. The poem originally possessed an additional verse, but, at the suggestion of Mrs. Whitman, this was subsequently omitted, and the effect of the whole thereby greatly strengthened.

Early in 1848, Poe announced his intention of delivering a series of lectures, with a view to raise a sufficient sum to enable him to start a magazine of his own; the magazine to be called "The Stylus," and to be "entirely out of the control of a publisher." To get the requisite number of subscribers he purposed, he wrote to Willis.

"To go South and West, among my personal and literary friends, old college and West Point acquaintances, and see what I can do. In order to get the means of taking the first step, I propose to lecture at the Society Library, on the 3d of February, and, that there may be no cause of *squabbling*, my subject shall *not be literary* at all. I have chosen a broad text—'The Universe.'"

The lecture was delivered in the library of the Historical Society; it was upon the cosmogony of the universe, and formed the substance of the work he afterward published as "Eureka, a Prose Poem." Mr. M. B. Field, who was present, says:

"It was a stormy night, and there were not more than sixty persons present in the lecture-room. . . His lecture was a rhapsody of the most intense brilliancy. He appeared inspired, and his inspiration affected the scant audience almost painfully. His eyes seemed to glow like those of his own 'Raven, and he kept us entranced for two hours and a half."

Such small audiences, despite the enthusiasm of the lecturer, or the lectured, could not give much material aid toward the poet's purpose. Poor and baffled, he had to return to his lonely home at Fordham to contemplate anew the problems of creation; or to discuss with stray visitors, with an intensity of feeling and steadfastness of belief never surpassed, his attempted unriddling of the secret of the universe.

Notwithstanding his many admirers, and the friendly co-operation of Mr. Thomas C. Clarke, of Philadelphia, who was to have been the publisher, Poe was unable to get the minimum number of subscribers necessary to start the magazine upon a sound basis; nor did his first lecture, as is palpable, render much assistance toward "the means of taking the first step." In the early summer of the same year, Poe lectured at Lowell, on the "Female Poets of America," and in the lecture paid some very high compliments to the "pre-eminence in refinement of art, enthusiasm, imagination, and genius" of Mrs. Whitman, certainly the finest female poet New England has yet produced. Griswold says Mrs. Whitman had first been seen by Poe.

"On his way from Boston, when he visited that city to deliver a poem before the Lyceum there. Restless, near midnight, he wandered from his hotel near where she lived, until he saw her walking in a garden. He related the incident afterward in one of his most exquisite poems, worthy of himself, of her, and of the most exalted passion."

But the lady was unconscious of the fierce flame she had aroused in the poet's heart, although, about the time of the above-named lecture, the first intimation reached her, in the shape of the exquisite lines "To Helen," alluded to by Griswold, commencing, "I saw thee once—once only—years ago." The poem was unsigned, but the lady had already seen Edgar Poe's exquisite handwriting, and knew, therefore, whence it came. In September, the poet, having obtained a letter of introduction from a lady friend, sought and obtained an interview with Mrs. Whitman. The result of this and several subsequent meetings was the betrothal of the two poets, but in the following December their engagement came to an end. The real cause of the rupture between Poe and his *fiancée* has never been published, but there is direct evidence of the utter falsity of the diabolical story repeated in nearly every memoir of the poet. On the evening before what should have been the bridal morn, says Griswold, Poe committed such drunken outrages at the house of his affianced bride, as rendered it necessary to summon the police to eject him, which, he remarks, of course ended the engagement. This mis-statement being brought under the notice of the parties concerned, Mr. William I. Pabodie, of Providence, Rhode Island, wrote a direct and specific denial of it, which appeared in the "New York Tribune," on the 7th of June 1852. "I am authorised to say," remarks Mr. Pabodie, who, it is scarcely necessary to mention, was a lawyer, as well as a man of considerable literary ability, "not only from my personal knowledge, but also from the statement of ALL who were conversant with the affair, that there exists not a shadow of foundation for the story above alluded to." The same letter goes on to state that its writer knew Poe well, and at the time alluded to was with him daily. "I was acquainted with the circumstances of his engagement, and with the causes which led to its dissolution," continues Mr. Pabodie; and he concludes his letter with an earnest appeal to Griswold to do all that now lies in his power "to remove an undeserved stigma from the memory of the departed." Griswold should have acknowledged that he had been mis-informed, and should have done his best to obviate the consequences of his accusation. Not so: he wrote a savage letter to Mr. Pabodie, threatening terrible things if he did not withdraw his statement. Mr. Pabodie *did not withdraw*, but in a second letter brought forward incontrovertible proofs of other falsifications indulged in by the author of the "Memoir," who remained, henceforward, discreetly silent.

During the larger portion of 1848, Poe continued his studies, which at this period were chiefly philosophical, at his home in Fordham. Beyond a few reviews and "Marginalia," he would appear to have given his whole time to the completion of " Eureka," the various knotty points of which last and grandest effort of his genius he was wont to descant upon with an eloquence that electrified his hearers into belief. He could not submit to hear the claims of his work coolly discussed by unsympathetic and incompetent critics, and after it was published in book form, and thus made public property, he addressed a stinging letter to the " Literary World," in reply to a flippant critique of the work which had appeared in the columns of that paper. The winter of 1848 and 1849, and the spring of the latter year, Poe passed at Fordham, and during this time he is alleged to have written a book entitled " Phases of American Literature "; and Mr. M. A. Daly states that he saw the complete work, but the manuscript would seem to have disappeared. After Poe's death the larger portion of his papers passed through Griswold's hands, and this will doubtless account for all deficiencies. In the summer, Poe revisited Richmond, and spent between two and three months there, during which time he delivered two lectures, in the Exchange Concert Room, on " The Poetic Principle."

"When in Richmond," says Mr. Thompson, "he made the office of the 'Messenger' a place of frequent resort. His conversation was always attractive, and at times very brilliant. Among modern authors his favorite was Tennyson, and he delighted to recite from 'The Princess' the song 'Tears, idle tears'—and a fragment of which,

"When unto dying eyes
The casement slowly grows a glimmering square,"

he pronounced unsurpassed by any image expressed in writing."

For Mr. Thompson, whom he inspired with an affection similar to that with which he inspired all with whom he had personal dealings, he wrote much of his sparkling and vivid "Marginalia," as well as reviews of "Stella" (Mrs. Lewis), and of Mrs. Osgood. To his probity and general worth Mr. Thompson, who saw so much of him in his latter days, bears feeling testimony. In 1853, writing to Mr. James Wood Davidson, the talented author of "Living Writers of the South," Mr. Thompson remarks:

"Two years ago, I had a long conversation in Florence, with Mr. Robert and Elizabeth Barrett Browning, concerning Poe. The two poets, like yourself, had formed an ardent and just admiration of the author of 'The Raven,' and feel a strong desire to see his memory vindicated from moral aspersion."

Unfortunately, the vindication has been slower than the aspersion to make its way in the world.

Edgar Poe had not been long in Richmond on this occasion of his final visit, before it was rumored that he was engaged to the love of his youth, Mrs. Shelton (née Royster), who was now a widow; but he never alluded in any way to such an engagement to his friend Thompson, intimate as he was with him. On the 4th of October he left Richmond by train, with the intention, it is supposed, of going to Fordham to fetch Mrs. Clemm. Before his departure he complained to a friend of indisposition, of chilliness, and of exhaustion, but nevertheless determined to undertake the journey. He left the cars at Baltimore, and several hours later was discovered in the streets insensible. How he was taken ill no one really knows, and *most* of the absurd reports circulated about his last moments must necessarily be absolute inventions. The most trustworthy account is that the unfortunate man was seized by a gang of ruffians, " cooped," stupefied with liquor, dragged to the polls, and having " voted the ticket placed in his hands," was then left in the street to die. When found he was in a dying state, and being unknown, was taken to the Washington University Hospital, where he died on Sunday the 7th of October, 1849, of inflammation of the brain. The following day his remains were buried in the burial-ground of Westminster church, close by the grave of his grandfather, General David Poe.

In telling the true story of Edgar Poe's life, it is impossible to utterly ignore the fact—a fact of which his enemies have made so much—that toward the close of his melancholy career, sorrow and pecuniary embarrassment drove him to the use of stimulants, as affording the only procurable nepenthe for his troubles. " A less delicate organisation than his," remarks one of his acquaintances, " might have borne without injury, what to him was maddening." " I have absolutely *no* pleasure in the stimulants in which I some-times so madly indulge," he wrote, some months before his death, to a dear friend who had tried to hold forth a saving hope. " It has not been in the pursuit of pleasure that I have perilled life and reputation and reason. It has been in the desperate attempt to escape from torturing memories—memories of wrong and injustice and imputed dishonor—from a sense of insupportable loneliness and a dread of some strange impending gloom." There is no necessity for us to touch heavily upon this terrible *trait* in the character of Edgar Poe—this sad, sickening infirmity of his " lonesome latter years ": his error, if such it may be styled—the impulse which blindly impelled him to his destruction—injured no one but himself; but certainly no one before or since has suffered so severely in character as a consequence of such a fault. Other children of genius have erred far worse than Poe ever did, inasmuch as their derelictions have injured others; but with them the world has dealt leniently, accepting *their* genius as a compensation. But for poor Edgar Poe, who wronged no one but himself, the world, misled greatly, it is true, as to his real character, has hitherto had no mercy. The true story of his life has now been told; henceforth let him be judged justly; henceforth let his errors be forgotten, and to his name be assigned that place which is due to it in the glory-roll of fame.

JOHN H. INGRAM.

Some Reminiscences of Edgar A. Poe
as a Schoolboy.

By Col. J. T. L. Preston.

MY recollections of Poe are very distinct; but they belong to so brief a space, and to so immature a period of his life, and to a still more immature one of my own, that in recalling them, they seem trivial.

Although I was several years his junior, we sat together on the same form, for a year or more, at a classical school in Richmond, Virginia. Our master was John Clark, of Trinity College, Dublin. At that time his school was the one of highest repute in the metropolis. One which was to become still more celebrated, under the guidance of Mr. Burke, was just then rising into notice.

Master Clark was a hot-tempered, pedantic, bachelor Irishman; but a Latinist of the first order, according to the style of scholarship of that date, he unquestionably was. I have often heard my mother amuse herself by repeating his pompous assurance, that in his school her boy should be taught "only the pure Latinity of the Augustan age." It is due to his memory to say, that if her boy was not properly grounded in his rudiments, it was not the fault of his teacher. What else we were taught I have forgotten; but my drilling in Latin, even to its minutiæ, is clear to my view as if lying on the surface of yesterday.

Edgar Poe might have been, at this time, fifteen or sixteen—he being one of the oldest boys in the school, and I one of the youngest. His power and accomplishments captivated me, and something in me or in him made him take a fancy to me. In the simple school athletics of those days, where a gymnasium had not been heard of, he was *facile princeps*. He was a swift runner, a wonderful leaper, and what was more rare, a boxer, with some slight training. I remember too, that he would allow the strongest boy in the school to strike him with full force in the chest. He taught me the secret, and I imitated him after my measure. It was, to inflate the lungs to the uttermost, and at the moment of receiving the blow, to exhale the air. It looked surprising, and was indeed a little rough; but with a good breast-bone and some resolution, it was not difficult to stand it. For swimming he was noted, being in many of his athletic proclivities surprisingly like Byron in his youth. There was no one among the schoolboys who would so dare in the midst of the rapids of the James River. I recall one of his races. A challenge to a foot-race had been passed between the two classical schools of the city. We selected Poe as our champion. The race came off one bright May morning at sunrise, on the Capitol Square. Historical truth compels me to add, that on this occasion our school was beaten, and we had to pay up our small bets. Poe ran well; but his competitor was a long-legged, Indian-looking fellow, who would have outstripped Atalanta without the help of the golden apple. Ah, how many of those young racers on Capitol Square that fair May morning, and how many of the crowd that so eagerly looked on, are very still now!

In our Latin exercises in school, Poe was among the first—not first without dispute. He had competitors who fairly disputed the palm. Especially one "Nat Howard," afterward known as one of the ripest scholars in Virginia, though distinguished also as a profound lawyer. If Howard was less brilliant than Poe, he was far more studious; for even then the germs of waywardness were

developing in the nascent poet, and even then no inconsiderable
portion of his time was given to versifying. But if I put Howard,
as a Latinist, on a level with Poe, I do him full justice. One
exercise of the school was a favorite one with Poe : it was what
was called " capping verses." The practice is so absolutely obsolete
now, at least in our country, that the term may require explanation.
Before the close of the school, all the Latinists, without regard to
age or respective advancement in the language, were drawn up in
a line for "capping verses": just as in old-fashioned schools, all
scholars had to take their place in the spelling-line before
dismission. At the head of the line stood the best scholar, who
gave, from memory, some verse of Latin poetry to be "capped":
that is, he challenged all the line to give, from memory, another
verse beginning with the same initial letter. Whoever was able
to do this took the place of the leader, and in his turn propounded
another verse, to be capped in like manner. This we called "simple
capping." " Double capping " was more difficult, inasmuch as the
responding verse must at once begin and also *end* with the same
letters as the propounded verse. To give an example, and at the
same time to illustrate how a memory, like a sieve, may let through
what is valuable, and yet retain on its reticulations a worthless
speck, I recall a capping which, while I have forgotten ten
thousand things that would have been serviceable if remembered,
comes back to me with distinctness after the lapse of so many
years. Nat Howard stood at the head of the line, and gave out
for " double capping " a verse beginning with the letter *d*, and
ending with the letter *m*. It passed Edgar Poe ; it passed other
good scholars, as well it might, until it reached me, a tiro away
down the line. To the surprise of everybody, and not less to my
own, there popped into my mind this line of Virgil :

Ducite ab urbe domum, mea carmina, ducite Daphnim—

and with pride and amazement I saw myself where I never was

before, and never was afterwards—above Nat Howard and Edgar Poe. This practice looks absurd, and so it would be now. True, it stored the memory with many good quotations for ready use; but what speaker would quote Latin now? And if scholars were required to commit Latin verse, where would be the time for learning such philosophy as, the genitive is the case of the lacking half, or that *ubi* is the ablative or the locative case of *qui?* But after the fashion of Master Clark, a fashion brought from Trinity, this "capping verses" was much in vogue, and Edgar Poe was an expert at it. He was very fond of the Odes of Horace, and repeated them so often in my hearing that I learned by sound the words of many, before I understood their meaning. In the lilting rhythm of the Sapphics and Iambics, his ear, as yet untutored in more complicated harmonics, took special delight. Two odes in particular have been humming in my ear all my life since, set to the tune of his recitation:

> Jam satis terris, nivis atque diræ
> Grandinis misit Pater et rubente—

and

> Non ebur neque aureum
> Mea renidet in domo lacunar, &c.

When I think of his boyhood, his career, and his fate, the poet whose lines I first learned from his musical lip, supplies me with his epitaph:

> Ille mordaci velut icta ferro
> Pinus, aut impulsa cupressus Euro,
> Procidit late, posuitque collum in
>   Pulvere Teucro.

I remember that Poe was also a very fine French scholar. Yet with all his superiorities, he was not the master-spirit, nor even the favorite of the school. I assign, from my recollection, this place to Howard. Poe, as I recall my impressions now, was self-willed, capricious, inclined to be imperious, and though of generous impulses, not steadily kind or even amiable ; and so what he would exact was refused to him. I add another thing which had its influence, I am sure. At the time of which I speak, Richmond was one of the most aristocratic cities on this side of the Atlantic. I hasten to say that this is not so now. Aristocracy (like capping verses) has fallen into desuetude—perhaps for the same reason : times having changed, other things pay better. Richmond was certainly then very English and very aristocratic. A school is, of its nature, democratic ; but still, boys will unconsciously bear about the odor of their fathers' notions, good or bad. Of Edgar Poe it was known that his parents were players, and that he was dependent upon the bounty that is bestowed upon an adopted son. All this had the effect of making the boys decline his leadership ; and on looking back on it since, I fancy it gave him a fierceness he would otherwise not have had. And, after all, was the instinct of boyhood mistaken ? Had Poe been better born and otherwise bred, could he have been just what he was, and what we would be glad to forget ?

Not a little of Poe's time, in school and out of it, was occupied with writing verses. As we sat together he would show them to me, and even sometimes ask my opinion, and now and then my assistance. I recall at this moment his consulting me about one particular line, as to whether the word *groat* would properly rhyme with such a word as *not*. It would not surprise me now if I should be able, by looking over his juvenile poems, to identify that very line. As it is my only chance for poetic fame, I must, I think, institute the search !

My boyish admiration was so great for my schoolfellow's genius, that I requested him to give me permission to carry his portfolio home for the inspection of my mother. If her enthusiasm was less than mine, her judgment did not hesitate to praise the verses very highly ; and her criticism might well gratify the boyish poet ; for she was a lady who, to a natural love for literature, inherited from her father, Edmund Randolph, had added the most thorough and careful culture obtained by the most extensive reading of the English classics—the established mode of female education in those days. Here, then, you have the first critic to whom were submitted the verses of our world-famed poet. Her warm appreciation of the boy's genius and work, was proof of her own critical taste.

As I have thus complied with the request you have made, pleasant echoes of those young and happy years have been falling upon my ear. A stern world may, with justice, find fault with the later life of the poet; and his biographer may regret the frailties and the sorrows he has to record; but my reminiscences are only the boyish memories of a morning hour before the shadows had arisen.

DEDICATION OF THE MONUMENT.

CEREMONIES OF THE OCCASION.

THE ceremonies connected with the dedication of the Poe Monument took place on November 17, 1875. The main hall of the Western Female High School was occupied by a large audience, ladies composing the major portion, some time before the hour set for the beginning of the exercises. The platform at the head of the hall was filled with a number of gentlemen, Principals of the High Schools, those who were to take part in the exercises, gentlemen who had been acquaintances or associates of the poetic genius in honor of whose memory the meeting was held, and other invited guests. Among them were Prof. John Hewitt, once editor of the *Saturday Visitor*, in which Poe's weird story of "The Manuscript Found in a Bottle" first appeared; Dr. John H. Snodgrass, also a former editor of the *Visitor*; Prof. N. C. Brooks, who edited the *American Magazine*, in which some of Poe's earliest productions appeared, and Prof. Joseph Clarke, a very venerable gentleman, whose school at Richmond, Virginia, had been attended by Poe when a boy. Among others on the platform were Prof. J. C. Kincar, of Pembroke Academy; Dr. N. H. Morison, Provost of Peabody Institute; John T. Morris, Esq., President of the School Board; the Rev. Dr. Julius E. Grammer, Judge Garey, Joseph Merrefield, Esq., Dr. John G. Morris, Neilson Poe, Esq., Ichabod Jean, Esq., Summerfield Baldwin, Joseph J. Stewart, Esq., Professors Thayer and Hollingshead,

John T. Ford, Esq., George Small, Esq., the Faculty of the Baltimore City College, M. A. Newell, State School Superintendent, as well as those who were to take part in the proceedings. The exercises began shortly after two o'clock with the performance of the "Pilgrim's Chorus" of Verdi, by the Philharmonic Society, who occupied raised seats in the rear of the hall, under the direction of Professor Remington Fairlamb.

At the close of the music Prof. William Elliott, Jr., President of the Baltimore City College, delivered the following address, containing

THE HISTORY OF THE MOVEMENT

culminating in the exercises of the day:

LADIES AND GENTLEMEN—I purpose, in discharging the duty assigned me on this occasion, to give a brief historical sketch of the movement which culminates to-day in the dedication of a monument to the memory of the great American poet, Edgar Allan Poe, the first and only memorial expression of the kind ever given to an American on account of literary excellence.

This extraordinary and unique genius, born in Boston, January 20th, 1809, during a brief sojourn of his parents in that place, died on the 7th of October, 1849, in this city, which is undoubtedly entitled to claim him as one of her distinguished sons. Two days thereafter, on the 9th of October, his mortal remains were interred in the cemetery attached to the Westminster Presbyterian Church, adjoining the building in which we are now assembled.

In this connection, acting as a truthful chronicler, I deem it proper to state some facts in relation to the circumstances of the interment. The reliability of the statement I shall now make is sufficiently attested by the evidence of at least three of the gentlemen present on that occasion—possibly the only three who yet survive.

I have been informed that the day was, for the season, more than ordinarily unpleasant, the weather being raw and cold; indeed, just such a day as it would have been more comfortable to spend within than without doors.

The time of the interment was about four o'clock in the afternoon; the attendance of persons at the grave, possibly a consequence of the state of the weather, was limited to eight, certainly to not more than nine, persons, one of these being a lady.

Of the number known to have been present were Hon. Z. Collius Lee, a classmate of the deceased at the University of Virginia; Henry Herring, Esq., a connection of Mr. Poe; Rev. W. T. D. Clemm, a relative of Mr. Poe's wife; our well-known fellow-citizen, Neilson Poe, Esq., a cousin of the poet; Edmund Smith, Esq., and wife, the latter being a first cousin ot Poe, and at this time his nearest living relative in this city, and possibly Dr. Snodgrass, the editor of the *Saturday Visitor*, the paper in which the prize-story written by Poe first made its appearance. The clergyman who officiated at the grave was Rev. W. T. D. Clemm, already mentioned, a member of the Baltimore Conference of the Methodist Episcopal Church, who read the impressive burial service used by that denomination of Christians, after which all that was mortal of Edgar Allan Poe was gently committed to its mother-earth.

Another item which it may not be inappropriate to record in this historical compend, I will now mention, namely, that George W. Spence, who officiated as sexton at the burial of Mr. Poe, is the same person who, after the lapse of twenty-six years, has superintended the removal of his remains, and those of his loving and beloved mother-in-law, Mrs. Clemm, and their reinterment in the lot in which the monument now stands.

For a number of years after the burial of the poet, no steps seem to have been taken towards marking his grave, until at length a stone was prepared for this purpose by order of Neilson Poe, Esq. Unfortunately, however, this stone never served the purpose for which it was designed. A train of cars accidentally ran into the establishment of Mr. Hugh Sisson, at which place the stone was at the time, and so damaged it as to render it unfit to be used as intended.

Another series of years intervened, but yet no movement to mark the grave. True, numerous articles made their appearance at short intervals during that time in different newspapers, but the authors of those articles were mostly of that class of persons who employ their energies in finding fault with others, totally oblivious of the fact that they themselves no less deserved the censure they so liberally mete out to others.

"Poe's neglected grave" was the stereotyped expression of these modern Jeremiahs. Nor were they content to indulge in lamentations; not unfrequently our good city was soundly berated because of its alleged want of appreciation of the memory of one whose ashes, they intimated, had he been an Englishman, instead of filling an unmarked grave in an obscure cemetery, would have had accorded to them a place in that grand old abbey which England has appropriated as a mausoleum for her distinguished dead.

But the "neglected grave" was not always to remain such. At a regular meeting of the Public School Teachers' Association, held in this hall, October 7, 1865, Mr. John Basil, Jr., Principal of No. 8 Grammar School, offered a paper, of which the following is a copy:

"*Whereas*, It has been represented to certain members of the Association that the mortal remains of Edgar Allan Poe are interred in the cemetery of the Westminster Church without even so much as a stone to mark the spot; therefore,

"*Resolved*, That a committee of five be appointed by the President of this Association to devise some means best adapted in their judgment to perpetuate the memory of one who has contributed so largely to American literature."

This resolution was unanimously adopted, and a committee, consisting of Messrs. Basil, Baird, and J. J. G. Webster, Miss Veeder and Miss Wise, appointed to carry out the purpose named.

This committee reported in favor of the erection of a monument, and recommended that measures be at once taken to secure the funds necessary to accomplish this object. This recommendation was heartily endorsed by the association, and without delay the committee entered upon the work of raising the funds.

In this work the young ladies of the Western Female High School took an active, and, as will be seen, a successful part. Two literary entertainments were given under the superintendence of Miss S. S. Rice, in 1865, to the proceeds of which were added a gift from Prof. Charles Davies, of New York, and one from the young ladies of Troy Female Seminary. The amount in the treasurer's hands, on March 23, 1871, was $587.02. The enthusiasm that characterised the undertaking at the outset seemed now to have greatly abated, and serious thoughts were consequently entertained of abandoning the project. At this juncture a new committee, consisting of Messrs. Elliott, Kerr and Hamilton, Miss Rice and Miss Baer, was appointed to consider the matter.

On April 13, 1872, this committee reported as follows: "First, resolved, that the money now in the hands of the treasurer of the 'Poe Memorial Fund' be appropriated to the erection of a monument, the same to be placed over Poe's remains. Second, that a committee of five be appointed by the President, with power to act as stated in the first resolution." These resolutions were adopted, and the committee therein provided for appointed, as follows: Wm. Elliott, Jr., A. S. Kerr, Alexander Hamilton, Miss S. S. Rice, and Miss E. A. Baer. September 2, 1874, this committee received from the estate of Dr. Thomas D. Baird, deceased, the late treasurer of the "Poe Memorial Fund," $627.55, the amount of principal and interest to that date, which was immediately deposited in the Chesapeake Bank, of this city. Believing that this amount could be increased to $1000 by donations from some of our fellow citizens who favored the project, the committee applied to Mr. George A. Frederick, architect of the City Hall, for a design of a monument to cost about that sum.

Mr. Frederick in due time submitted a design "at once simple, chaste and dignified," but requiring for its realisation much more than the amount included in the expectations of the committee. Moreover, a new feature was now introduced, that of placing a medallion likeness of the poet on one of the panels of the monument, which would still further increase the cost. With a view of determining whether the amount necessary to complete the monument according to the proportions it had now assumed could be raised, applications were made to a number of our citizens for contributions. From one of acknowledged æsthetic taste a check of $100 was promptly received, and $153 were given in small sums.

The known liberality of Mr. George W. Childs, of Philadelphia, formerly one of our fellow-townsmen, induced the Chairman of the committee to drop him a note on the subject. Within twenty-four hours a reply was received from that gentleman expressive of his willingness to make up the estimated deficiency of $650.

The necessary amount having now been secured, the committee proceeded to place the construction and erection of the monument in the hands of Mr. Hugh Sisson, his proposal being the most liberal one received. How faithfully he has executed his commission will be seen when the covering that now veils the monument is removed. No one so well as the Chairman of the committee knows how anxious Mr. Sisson has been to meet even more than the expectations of those most concerned. To his generous liberality are we largely indebted for the reproduction of the classic lineaments of the poet in the beautiful and highly artistic medallion that adds so much to the attractiveness of the monument.

To most of those present, I presume, it is known that the lot in which the monument is now located is not the one in which it was first placed. In deference to what was considered by the committee the popular wish, the monument was removed from its first location to its present one. The remains of Mr. Poe, and also those of his mother-in-law, were, as before intimated, removed at the same time. The new lot was secured mainly through the efforts of Mr. John T. Morris, President of the School Board, to whom and to all others who have in any way contributed to the consummation of this undertaking, I wish here, on behalf of the committee, to render thanks.*

In conclusion, allow me to congratulate all concerned that Poe's grave is no longer a neglected one

Upon the conclusion of Professor Elliott's address, which was listened to with deep interest, Miss Sara S. Rice was introduced to the audience. To this lady, well known to the public from her elocutionary attainments, the greatest possible credit is due for the

---

* The ground occupied by the monument covers parts of lots 171 and 180, belonging to the descendants of Mr. Robert Wilson and Mr. Alexander Fridge, whose representatives kindly gave permission for its use.

successful completion of the enterprise. The first money raised for the erection of the monument was through her personal efforts, and the entire movement, from its inception to the close, has enjoyed the benefit of her unremitting attention and effort. Miss Rice read various letters from poets and others, in response to invitations to be present on the occasion. (These will be found in another part of this volume.)

After the conclusion of the letters, the following poem, contributed by the well-known dramatic critic and *littérateur*, Mr. William Winter, was read by Miss Rice with exquisite delicacy and utterance, and received with a burst of applause:

AT POE'S GRAVE.

Cold is the pæan honor sings,
  And chill is glory's icy breath,
And pale the garland memory brings
  To grace the iron doors of death.

Fame's echoing thunders, long and loud,
  The pomp of pride that decks the pall,
The plaudits of the vacant crowd—
  One word of love is worth them all.

With dews of grief our eyes are dim;
  Ah, let the tear of sorrow start,
And honor, in ourselves and him,
  The great and tender human heart!

Through many a night of want and woe
  His frenzied spirit wandered wild—
Till kind disaster laid him low,
  And Heaven reclaimed its wayward child.

Through many a year his fame has grown,—
  Like midnight, vast, like starlight sweet,—
Till now his genius fills a throne,
  And nations marvel at his feet.

One meed of justice long delayed,
  One crowning grace his virtues crave:—
Ah, take, thou great and injured shade,
  The love that sanctifies the grave!

God's mercy guard in peaceful sleep,
The sacred dust that slumbers here;
And, while around *this tomb we weep,*
God bless, for us, the mourner's tear!

And may his spirit, hovering nigh,
Pierce the dense cloud of darkness through,
And know, with fame that cannot die,
He has the world's affection too!

The Philharmonic Society then rendered the grand chorus, "He Watcheth over Israel," from the "Elijah" of Mendelssohn, with fine effect.

ADDRESS UPON THE GENIUS AND LITERARY CHARACTER OF POE.

Prof. H. E. Shepherd was then introduced to the audience and delivered the following address:

LADIES AND GENTLEMEN—It is my purpose to speak of Edgar A. Poe principally as a poet and as a man of genius. I shall abstain, for the most part, from personal incidents or biographical details. These, though not devoid of interest, properly pertain to the historian of literature or to the biographer. Let his "strange eventful history" be reserved for some American Boswell, Masson or Morley.

Edgar A. Poe was born in 1809, the same year with Alfred Tennyson, the present Poet laureate, and with Mrs. Browning, the most gifted poetess of any age. The third great era in English literature had then fairly commenced. The glory of the elder day was revived. The delusive splendor that had so long gilded the Augustan age of Anne paled before the comprehensive culture, the marvellous intellectual expansion that distinguished the first thirty years of the present century. The spirit of poesy, no longer circumscribed by the arbitrary and enervating procedures of Dryden's contemplated academy, ranged in unchecked freedom over seas and continents, arousing the buried forms of mediæval civilisation, the lay of the minstrel, the lyric of the troubadour, the ancient splendor of the Arthurian cycle. One day was as a thousand years in the growth and advancement of the human mind. Edgar was in his childhood when the Georgian era had attained the full meridian of its greatness. He spent five years at school in England, from 1816 to 1821. During this interval little is known of his personal history, save what he has left us in the story of "William Wilson," in which he depicts, with a power of vivid delineation worthy of the best days of De Quincey, his impressions of the school and its surroundings. We may feel assured, however, that his mind was rapidly unfolding, and with that keen susceptibility characteristic of the dawning intellect of youth, acquiring a permanent coloring from the wonderful drama that was enacting around him. The term of Edgar's school-life in England was a period of intense poetical activity and creative power, heroic emprise, knightly valor and brilliant achievement. The atmosphere was vocal with the strains of songsters, whose notes make as sweet music as when they fell for the first time upon the ears of our youthful poet, and aroused him to the consciousness of poetic power. Alfred Tennyson was seven years of age when Edgar arrived in England, and during the time of Edgar's school-life at Stokes was spending his play-hours with Mallory's Morte D'Arthur upon his knees, musing upon the faded splendors of the Table Ronde, and looking forward, with prophetic vision, to the time when Lancelot, Arthur, Percival, and Galahad should regain their ancient sway, with more than their ancient renown as the mythical heroes of the British race. Mrs. Browning, and Arthur Hallam, the hero of "In Memoriam," were in their childhood; Byron, Scott, Shelley and Keats were in the zenith of their fame, and the English tongue had not been illustrated by so brilliant a constellation of poets since "the spacious times of great Elizabeth." It were difficult to imagine that this constellation did not exert an inspiring influence upon the genius and temperament of our youthful poet—an influence which must have in some degree determined his future career. He must have listened with that exquisite sympathy of which the poetic temperament alone is capable, to the mournful story of Keats, the "young Lycidas" of our poetic history. A strange resemblance in intellectual constitution may be discerned between these wayward children of genius—the same deep taint of Celtic melancholy; the same enthusiastic worship of supernal beauty; the same relentless struggle with the immutability of fact. The delicately wrought sensibilities of Keats, who "could feel the daisies growing over him," strikingly recalls the memory of our own poet, who imagined that he could "distinctly hear the darkness as it stole over the horizon." "A thing of beauty is a joy forever" was the animating principle of the genius of the one and the art of the other. In 1822, Edgar, then in his fourteenth year, returned to his native land. He attained to manhood at a time when, by a transition familiar in the history of every literature, the supremacy was reverting from poetry to prose. The Romanic fervor, the Spenserian symphonies of our last great poetic era, were gradually yielding to the steady advance of philological investigation, critical dissertation and scientific analysis. A new reflective era, more brilliant than that of Pope or Bolingbroke, was dawning. The cold generalisations of reason, the relentless inductions of philosophy, chilled the glowing ardor of the preceding era. The publication of Macaulay's essay on Milton in 1825 marked the transition from the sway of the imaginative faculty to the present unsurpassed period in our prose literature. From this desultory outline of nearly contemporary literature you will observe that our poet's intellectual constitution was formed under peculiar conditions. He does not belong chronologically to the Georgian era; his position was, for the most part, one of comparative isolation—like that of Sackville, Wyatt or Collins, in the midst of an unpoetic generation, unsustained by the consolations of poetic association or the tender endearments of poetic sympathy. When Poe attained to the full consciousness of his great powers, none of these quickening influences existed, save as matters of history or poetic tradition. Tennyson, in England, was viewing nature in perspective, and involving his critics in webs as tangled and hopeless as that which enveloped the fated Lady of Shallot. Wordsworth had abjured the teachings of his early manhood. Shelley, Keats and Byron were dead, Morris and Swinburne were yet unborn, and the thrones of the elder gods were principally filled by "the idle singers of an empty day." American poetry had then accomplished little that future ages will not willingly let die. The succession of sweet songsters is never entirely broken. The silver cord that binds in perennial union the spirit of Chaucer and the muse of Spenser is never severed, however slight and impalpable may be the filaments that bind it together. There are always some who retain the echoes of long-gone melodies, upon whom descends something of the inspiration of those grand epochs around which is concentrated so much of the glory of the English tongue. Such a position is not an anomaly in our literary history; such a relation was sustained by the chivalric Surrey, who introduced into the discordant English of his time that peculiar form of verse which was attuned to the harmonies of Milton, and by means of which Shakspeare, after a long and painful struggle with the "bondage of rhyming," rose to the supreme heights of poetic excellence. A similar relation was sustained by Sackville, the sombre splendor of whose "Induction" proved him the worthy herald of Spenser's dawning greatness; and the gentle Cowper, who marks the transition from the school of Johnson and of Addison, to the advent of the Gothic revival. Such was in some essential respects the position that Poe occupies among American poets in the order of poetic succession. Having traced somewhat in detail the conditions of the age during which our poet's intellectual constitution was developed, we are now prepared to appreciate the distinctive characteristics of his genius, as revealed in his prose, but more especially in his poetry. It is known to students of our literary history that in all periods of our literature, from the time that our speech was reduced to comparative uniformity by the delicate discrimination and rare philological perception of Chaucer, there have existed two recognised schools of poets, the native and the classical. In some, the classical element is the informing principle, as in Milton, whose pages, sprinkled with the diamond-dust of classic lore,—

52

"Thick as autumnal leaves that strew the brooks
In Vallombrosa,"

afford the most conspicuous illustration of its power. A wonderful impulse was communicated to the development of literary poetry by "that morning-star of modern song," the poet Keats, and since his advent our poetry has tended more and more to divest itself of native and domestic sympathies, and to assume an artistic character. Our poetry may have lost pliancy, but it has gained in elaboration and in verbal minuteness. Genius and imagination are not subdued, but are regulated by the canons of art, and from this harmonious alliance arises the unsurpassed excellence of the poetry of Poe. In the school of literary poets he must be ranked in that illustrious procession of bards which includes the names of Surrey, Shelley, Milton, Tennyson, Ben Jonson, Herrick, Cowley and Keats. Having assigned to Poe an honorable eminence in the goodly company of our literary poets, I proceed to speak of the originality, the creative power displayed in his poetry, as well as of his brilliant achievements in metrical composition.

Specific points of resemblance may be seen between his poetry and that of his predecessors and contemporaries, but no general or well defined likeness. There are individual traits that remind us of Marlowe, Greene, Byron, Shelley and Keats, but these are rather moral and mental coincidences than the impress or influence of mind upon mind. Few poets have displayed a more surpassing measure of creative power. Some of his maturer poems are almost without a precedent, in form as well as in spirit. The legend of the Raven, related by Roger De Hoveden, and referring to the era of the Latin conquest of Constantinople, nor the legend of Herod Agrippa, cited by De Quincey in his celebrated essay on modern superstition, furnishes an adequate foundation for the test of Poe's masterpiece. The raven has constituted a prominent character in English poetry for many years. In Macbeth, in Hamlet, in Sir David Lyndsay, in Tickell's exquisite ballad of Colin and Lucy, and in Coleridge, the appearance of this "ominous bird of yore" will suggest itself to all lovers of our dramatic and lyric poetry. But none of these can be considered as the precursor of Poe's poem. The nearest approach to any distinctive feature of the Raven is to be found, I suspect, in the dramas of Shakspeare, those unfailing sources of intellectual nutriment. The one word "Mortimer" of Harry Percy's starling presents a marked phonetic resemblance to the one word "Nevermore" of the Raven, whose melancholy refrain seems almost the echo of the starling's unvarying note. No poem in our language presents a more graceful grouping of metrical appliances and devices. The power of peculiar letters is evolved with a magnificent touch; the sonorous melody of the liquids is a characteristic feature not only of the refrain, but throughout the compass of the poem their "linked sweetness long drawn out" falls with a mellow cadence, displaying the poet's mastery of those mysterious harmonies which lie at the basis of human speech. The alliteration of the Norse minstrel and the Saxon bard, the skilful disposition of the caesural pauses, the continuity of the rhythm, illustrating Milton's ideal of "true musical delight," in which the sense is variously drawn out from one verse to another, the power of sustained interest, are some of the features that place the Raven foremost among the creations of poetic art in our age and clime. There are few more impressive examples of graphic and presentative power than the memorable lines:

> "And each separate, dying ember,
> Wrought its ghost upon the floor."

The intensity and vividness of the description are worthy of Milton, and call up to memory the celebrated lines of Il Penseroso, in which the contemplative spirit is represented as shunning the busy haunts of men, seeking some "loneliness unbroken" far from all resort of mirth—

> "Where glowing embers through the room,
> Teach light to counterfeit a gloom."

But perhaps the especial glory of the Raven is the originality of its metrical combinations. In the novelty of his metrical forms Poe has surpassed almost every poet of our era except Tennyson, as is frankly acknowledged by the English reviewers and eulogists of the Poet-laureate. The invention of new metres is a task upon which few poets have ventured for centuries. From Surrey to Cowley was an era of transition and experiment. Under the ascendancy of the conventional school our poetry glided smoothly and mechanically along in the orthodox ten-syllabled couplet, until Cowper broke through the consecrated forms of Dryden and Pope with a boldness and originality to which our literature had long been a stranger. Few of the poets of the Lake school ventured into the enchanted ground of metrical experiment. They were ofttimes inclined to discard the restraints of verse, or at least to render them subordinate to the spontaneous expression of the thought. With the advent of the new poetic school the increased attention to artistic elaboration, the expanding of our metrical forms became a question of serious import. The possible combinations of metre are infinite, but "for centuries," to use Poe's own language, "no man had thought of doing an original thing in verse." "The Raven," which is a novel blending of trochaic octometers, finding its nearest approach in the measure of "Lady Geraldine's Courtship," is one of the most brilliant achievements that our era has witnessed, and chronicles an epoch in the history of the metric art. In no department of his art is the genius of our poet more signally displayed than in his "Essay upon the Poetic Principle," in which the delicate and abstruse æsthetics of poetry are discussed with a masterly comprehension, and a felicity of illustration that entitle the author to be ranked among the most consummate critics that have ever lived. I have often thought that a dissertation upon poetry by a great poet would constitute an invaluable addition to the critical resources of our literature. But most illustrious masters have contented themselves with concrete examples, leaving the scholiasts and rhetoricians the irksome process of deducing theories of poetic diction from the models which they have presented. Oh, that Shakspeare had left us one line indicating the processes of his mind in the creation of Lear or of Cymbeline, or that Milton had bequeathed the rich legacy of a single item respecting the composition of "L'Allegro, or the Masque of Comus." But it is one of the signal benefits conferred upon the poetic literature of our tongue by E. A. Poe that he has transmitted to us a critical exposition of the principles of his art, which in correctness of conception, perspicuity and æsthetic sensibility is unsurpassed, perhaps unrivalled, in our language. A diligent reading of the "Essay" will reveal the fact that in his conceptions of poetry the mind of Poe was in perfect sympathy with the greatest masters of his own art, as well as with the most acute and discriminating expositors of the art of criticism. His theory of poetry is in thorough accord with that of Shakspeare as revealed in the few invaluable suggestions he has left us in the "Midsummer Night's Dream," and in a single line in the play of "As You Like It." It is repeated in terms almost identical by Shakspeare's contemporary, Sir Francis Bacon, in his "Advancement of Learning." "When I am asked for a definition of poetry," Poe wrote to a friend, "I think of 'Titania,' of 'Oberon,' of the 'Midsummer Night's Dream' of Shakspeare." The most distinguishing characteristic of Poe's poetry is its rhythmical power, and its admirable illustration of that mysterious affinity which links together the sound and the sense. Throughout all the processes of creation, a rhythmical movement is clearly discernible. Upon the conscious recognition of this principle are based all our conceptions of melody, all systems of intonation and inflection. In this dangerous sphere of poetic effort he attained a mastery over the properties of verse that the Troubadours might have aspired to imitate.

I would next direct your attention to the classic impress of Poe's poetry, its felicitous blending of genius and culture, and to the estimation in which his poetry is held in other lands. The Attic sculptor in the palmiest days of Athenian art, wrought out his loveliest conceptions by the painful processes of unflagging diligence. The angel was not evoked from the block by a sudden inspiration, or a brilliant flash of unpremeditated art. By proceeding upon a system corresponding to the diatonic scale in music, the luxuriance of genius was regulated by the sober precepts and decorous graces of formal art. No finer illustration of conscious art has been produced in our era than the Raven. In all the riper productions of our poet there is displayed the same consummate artistic taste. He attained a graceful mastery over the subtle and delicate metrical forms, even those to whose successful production the spirit of the English tongue is not congenial. The sonnet, that peculiarly Italian type of verse immortalised by the genius of Petrarch, has been admirably illustrated in Poe's poem of Zante. Indeed, much of the acrimony of his criticisms arose from his painful sensitiveness to artistic imperfection, and his enthusiastic worship of sensuous beauty. The Grecian cast of his genius led to a pantheistic love of the beautiful embodied in palpable or material types. This striving after purely sensuous beauty has formed a distinctive characteristic of those poets who were most thoroughly imbued with the Grecian taste and spirit. They have left their impress deep upon the texture of our poesy, and many of its most silvery symphonies owe their inspiration to this source. In addition to the classic element, his poetry is pervaded by that natural magic of style, that strange unrest and unreality, those weird notes, like the refrain of his own Raven, "so musical, so melancholy," which are traceable to the Celtic influence upon our composite intellectual character. The quick sensibility, the ethereal temper of these natural artists have wonderfully enlivened the stolid character of our Anglo-Saxon ancestors; and much of the style and constructive power that have reigned in English poetry since the days of Walter Map, of Layamon, and Chaucer, may be justly attributed to the Celtic infusion into the Teutonic blood. Conspicuous illustrations of its power may be discovered in Shakspeare, in Keats, in Byron and in Poe. I have thus endeavored to present to you the poetic and intellectual character of Poe as it has revealed itself to me from the diligent study of his works, and from many contrasts and coincidences which literary history naturally suggests. I have endeavored to show the versatile character of his genius, the consummate as well as conscious art of his poetry, the graceful blending of the creative and the critical faculty, his want of deference to prototypes or models, the chaste and scholarly elegance of his diction, the Attic smoothness and the Celtic magic of his style. Much of what he has written may not preserve its freshness, or stand the test of critical scrutiny in after-times; but when subjected to the severest ordeal of varying fashion, popular caprice, "the old order changing, yielding place to new," there is much that will perish only with the English language. The riper productions of our poet, "The Raven," "Annabel Lee," the poem "To Helen," have received the most glowing tributes from the dispassionate critics of the old world. I shall ever remember the thrill of grateful appreciation with which I read the splendid eulogium upon the genius of Poe in the London *Quarterly Review*, in which he is ranked far above his contemporaries, and pronounced one of the most consummate artists of modern times, potentially the greatest critic of our era, and possessing perhaps the finest ear for rhythm that was ever formed. You are doubtless familiar with the impression produced by the Raven upon the mind of Mrs. Browning, "Shakspeare's daughter and Tennyson's sister." It is only of late that Algernon Swinburne, one of the master-spirits of the new poetic school, has accorded to Poe the pre-eminence among American poets. Alfred Tennyson has recently expressed his admiration of our poet, who, with true poetic ken, was among the first to appreciate the novelty and the difficulty of his method, and who, at a time when the Laureate's fame was obscured by adverse and undiscerning criticism, clearly foresaw the serene splendor of his matured greatness. An appreciative and generous Englishman has recently added to the literature of our language a superb edition of Poe's works, in which ample recognition is accorded to his rare and varied powers, and the calumnies of his acrimonious biographer are refuted by evidence that cannot be gainsaid or resisted. No reader of English periodical literature can fail to notice the frequent tributes to his genius, the numerous allusions to his memory, the impressive parallelisms between Poe and Marlowe, the contemporary of Shakspeare and Greene, the rival of the great dramatist, that have appeared in the columns of the *Athenæum*, the *Academy*, the British Quarterlies, and the transactions of the new Shakspeare Society. Nor is this lofty estimate of his powers confined to those lands in which the English language is the vernacular speech; it has extended into foreign climes, and aroused appreciative admiration where English literature is imperfectly known and slightly regarded. Let us rejoice that at last Poe's merits have found appropriate recognition among his own countrymen, and that the Poet's Corner in our Westminster is rescued from the ungrateful neglect which for a quarter of a century has constituted the just reproach of our State and metropolis. In the dedication of this monument to the memory of our poet, I recognise an omen of highest and noblest import, reaching far beyond the mere preservation of his fame by the " dull, cold marble " which marks his long-neglected grave. The impulse which led to its erection coincides in spirit and character with those grand movements which the zeal and enthusiasm of patriots and scholars in Great Britain and America have effected within the past ten years for the perpetuation of much that is noblest in the poesy of the English tongue. At last we have the works of Geoffrey Chaucer restored to their original purity by the praiseworthy diligence of Furnival, Morris, and Bradshaw. At last we are to add to the golden treasures of our literature, genuine editions of Shakspeare, in which the growth of his genius and his art will be traced by the graceful scholarship and penetrating insight of Tennyson, Ingleby, Browning, Spedding and Simpson. Ten years have accomplished what centuries failed to achieve in rescuing from strange and unpardonable indifference the masterpieces of our elder literature, the Sibylline leaves of our ancient poesy. This graceful marble, fit emblem of our poet, is the expression, unconscious and undesigned, but none the less effective, of sympathy with this grand intellectual movement of our era. I hail these auspicious omens of the future of our literature with gratitude and delight; but while we welcome these happy indications, while we rejoice in the critical expansion of our peerless literature, let us not disregard the solemn injunction conveyed by this day's proceedings. While we pay these last tributes of regard to the memory of him who alone was worthy among American poets to be ranked in that illustrious procession of bards, among whose names is concentrated so much of the glory of the English tongue from Chaucer to Tennyson, let us cherish the admonition to nurture and stimulate the genius of poetry in our land, until it ascend "with no middle flight" into the "brightest heaven of invention" and the regions of purest phantasy.

Professor Shepherd was frequently interrupted with applause during the delivery of his eloquent address. Poe's famous poem of "The Raven" was then read, after which the *Inflammatus* from the *Stabat Mater* of Rossini was rendered by the Philharmonic Society, Miss Ella Gordon sustaining the solo passages.

REMINISCENCES OF POE BY JOHN H. B. LATROBE.

John H. B. Latrobe, Esq., was then introduced and delivered the following address:

LADIES AND GENTLEMEN—It has been announced that I am to give to this meeting "my personal recollections" of the great poet whose name has attracted the crowd before me. The inference from such an announcement would be that my acquaintance was such as to enable me to describe him as one friend or close acquaintance has it in his power to describe another. You may be surprised, then, when I say that I never saw Edgar Allan Poe but once, and that our interview did not last an hour. Those, therefore, who invited me to be present here to-day, gave to my assent a scope which was not justified by what I said, or to what it was in my power to do. The opportunity is afforded, however, of narrating the circumstances that led to our brief interview, and of correcting misstatements in regard, as it turned out, to a not unimportant event of his life. In adding an account of what occurred when we met, I shall have excused myself for taking the liberty, under the circumstances, of appearing before you at all.

About the year 1832 there was a newspaper in Baltimore called *The Saturday Visitor*—an ephemeral publication, that aimed at amusing its readers with light literary productions rather than the news of the day. One of its efforts was to procure original tales, and to this end it offered on this occasion two prizes, one for the best story and the other for the best short poem—one hundred dollars for the first and fifty dollars for the last. The judges appointed by the editor of the *Visitor* were the late John P. Kennedy, Dr.

James H. Miller (now deceased), and myself, and accordingly we met, one pleasant afternoon, in the back parlor of my house, on Mulberry street, and seated round a table garnished with some old wine and some good cigars, commenced our critical labors. As I happened then to be the youngest of the three, I was required to open the packages of prose and poetry, respectively, and read the contents. Alongside of me was a basket to hold what we might reject.

I remember well that the first production taken from the top of the prose pile was in a woman's hand, written very distinctly, as, indeed, were all the articles submitted, and so neatly that it seemed a pity not to award to it a prize. It was ruthlessly criticised, however, for it was ridiculously bad—namby-pamby in the extreme—full of sentiment and of the school known as the Laura Matilda school. The first page would have consigned it to the basket as our critical guillotine beheaded it. Gallantry, however, caused it to be read through, when in it went along with the envelope containing the name of the writer, which, of course, remained unknown. The next piece I have no recollection of, except that a dozen lines consigned it to the basket. I remember that the third, perhaps the fourth, production was recognised as a translation from the French, with a terrific denouement. It was a poor translation too; for, falling into literal accuracy, the writer had, in many places, followed the French idioms. The story was not without merit, but the Sir Fretful Plagiary of a translator deserved the charge of Sheridan in the *Critic*, of being like a beggar who had stolen another man's child and clothed it in his own rags. Of the remaining productions I have no recollection. Some were condemned after a few sentences had been read. Some were laid aside for reconsideration—not many. These last failed to pass muster afterwards, and the committee had about made up their minds that there was nothing before them to which they would award a prize, when I noticed a small quarto-bound book that had until then accidentally escaped attention, possibly because so unlike, externally, the bundles of manuscript that it had to compete with. Opening it, an envelope with a motto corresponding with one in the book appeared, and we found that our prose examination was still incomplete. Instead of the common cursive manuscript, the writing was in Roman characters—an imitation of printing. I remember that while reading the first page to myself, Mr. Kennedy and the Doctor had filled their glasses and lit their cigars, and when I said that we accidentally escaped attention, possibly of awarding the prize, they laughed as though they doubted it, and settled themselves in their comfortable chairs as I began to read. I had not proceeded far before my colleagues became as much interested as myself. The first tale finished, I went to the second, then to the next, and did not stop until I had gone through the volume, interrupted only by such exclamations as "capital!" "excellent!" "how odd!" and the like, from my companions. There was genius in everything they listened to; there was no uncertain grammar, no feeble phraseology, no ill-placed punctuation, no worn-out truisms, no strong thought elaborated into weakness. Logic and imagination were combined in rare consistency. Sometimes the writer created in his mind a world of his own and then described it—a world so weird, so strange—

> " Far down by the dim lake of Auber,
> In the misty mid-region of Wier;
> Far down by the dank tarn of Auber,
> In the ghoul-haunted woodland of Wier."

And withal so fascinating, so wonderfully graphic, that it seemed for the moment to have all the truth of a reality. There was an analysis of complicated facts—an unravelling of circumstantial evidence that won the lawyer judges—an amount of accurate scientific knowledge that charmed their accomplished colleague—a pure classic diction that delighted all three.

When the reading was completed there was a difficulty of choice. Portions of the tales were read again, and finally the committee selected " A MS. Found in a Bottle." One of the series was called " A Descent into the Maelström," and this was at one time preferred. I cannot now recall the names of all the tales—there must have been six or eight—but all the circumstances of the selection ultimately made have been so often since referred to in conversation that my memory has been kept fresh, and I see my fellow-judges over their wine and cigars, in their easy chairs—both genial, hearty men, in pleasant mood, as distinctly now as though I were describing an event of yesterday.

Having made the selection and awarded the one hundred dollar prize, not, as has been said, most unjustly and ill-naturedly, because the manuscript was legible, but because of the unquestionable genius and great originality of the writer, we were at liberty to open the envelope that identified him, and there we found in the note, whose motto corresponded with that of the little volume, the name, which I see you anticipate, of Edgar Allan Poe.

The statement in Dr. Griswold's life prefixed to the common edition of Poe's works, that " It was unanimously decided by the committee that the prize should be given to the first genius who had written legibly; not another MS. was unfolded," is absolutely untrue.

Refreshed by this most unexpected change in the character of the contributions, the committee refilled their glasses and relit their cigars, and the reader began upon the poetry. This, although better in the main than the prose, was bad enough, and, when we had gone more or less thoroughly over the pile of manuscript, two pieces only were deemed worthy of consideration. The title of one was " The Coliseum," the written printing of which told that it was Poe's. The title of the other I have forgotten, but, upon opening the accompanying envelope, we found that the author was Mr. John H. Hewitt, still living in Baltimore, and well known, I believe, in the musical world, both as a poet and composer. I am not prepared to say that the committee may not have been biased in awarding the fifty dollar prize to Mr. Hewitt by the fact that they had already given the one hundred dollar prize to Mr. Poe. I recollect, however, that we agreed that, under the circumstances, the excellence of Mr. Hewitt's poem deserved a reward, and we gave the smaller prize to him with clear consciences.

I believe that up to this time not one of the committee had ever seen Mr. Poe, and it is my impression that I was the only one that ever heard of him. When his name was read I remembered that on one occasion Mr. Wm. Gwynn, a prominent member of the bar of Baltimore, had shown me the very neat manuscript of a poem called " Al Aaraaf," which he spoke of as indicative of a tendency to anything but the business of matter-of-fact life. Those of my hearers who are familiar with the poet's works will recollect it as one of his earlier productions. Although Mr. Gwynn, being an admirable lawyer, was noted as the author of wise and witty epigrams in verse, " Al Aaraaf" was not in his vein, and what he said of the writer had not prepared me for the productions before the committee. His name, I am sure, was not at the time a familiar one.

The next number of the *Saturday Visitor* contained the " MS. Found in a Bottle," and announced the author. My office, in these days, was in the building still occupied by the Mechanics' Bank, and I was seated at my desk on the Monday following the publication of the tale, when a gentleman entered and introduced himself as the writer, saying that he came to thank me, as one of the committee, for the award in his favor. Of this interview, the only one I ever had with Mr. Poe, my recollection is very distinct indeed, and it requires but a small effort of imagination to place him before me now, as plainly almost as I see any one of my audience. He was, if anything, below the middle size, and yet could not be described as a small man. His figure was remarkably good, and he carried himself erect and well, as one who had been trained to it. He was dressed in black, and his frock-coat was buttoned to the throat, where it met the black stock, then almost universally worn. Not a particle of white was visible. Coat, hat, boots and gloves had very evidently seen their best days, but so far as mending and brushing go, everything had been done, apparently, to make them presentable. On most men his clothes would have looked shabby and seedy, but there was something about this man that prevented one from criticising his garments, and the details I have mentioned were only recalled afterwards. The impression made, however, was that the award in Mr. Poe's favor was not inopportune. *Gentleman* was written all over him. His manner was easy and quiet, and although he came to return thanks for what he regarded as deserving them, there was nothing obsequious in what he said or did. His features I am unable to describe in detail. His forehead was high and remarkable for the great development at the temple. This was the characteristic of his head, which you noticed at once, and which I have never forgotten. The expression of his face was grave, almost sad, except when he was engaged in conversation, when it became animated and changeable. His voice, I remember, was very pleasing in its tone and well modulated, almost rhythmical, and his words were well chosen and unhesitating. Taking a seat, we conversed a while on ordinary topics, and he informed me that Mr. Kennedy, my colleague in the committee, on whom he had already called, had either given, or promised to give him, a letter to the *Southern Literary Messenger*, which he hoped would procure him employment. I asked him whether he was then occupied with any literary labor. He replied that he was engaged on a voyage to the moon, and at once went into a somewhat learned disquisition upon the laws of gravity, the height of the earth's atmosphere and the capacities of balloons, warming in his speech as he proceeded. Presently, speaking in the first person, he began the voyage, after describing the preliminary arrangements, as you will find them set forth in one of his tales, called "The Adventure of one Hans Pfaall," and leaving the earth, and becoming more and more animated, he described his sensation, as he ascended higher and higher, until, at last, he reached the point in space where the moon's attraction overcame that of the earth, when there was a sudden bouleversement of the car and a great confusion among its tenants. By this time the speaker had become so excited, spoke so rapidly, gesticulating much, that when the turn-up-side-down took place, and he clapped his hands and stamped with his foot by way of emphasis, I was carried along with him, and, for aught to the contrary that I now remember, may have fancied myself the companion of his aerial journey. The climax of the tale was the reversal I have mentioned. When he had finished his description he apologised for his excitability, which he laughed at himself. The conversation then turned upon other subjects, and soon afterward he took his leave. I never saw him more. Dr. Griswold's statement "that Mr. Kennedy accompanied him (Poe) to a clothing store and purchased for him a respectable suit, with a change of linen, and sent him to a bath," is a sheer fabrication.

That I heard of him again and again, and year after year, in common with all English-speaking people, more and more, it is unnecessary to say—heard of him in terms of praise sometimes, sometimes in terms of censure, as we all have done, until now, that he has passed away, leaving his fame behind him, to last while our language lasts, I have grown to think of him only as the author who gave to the world the "Raven" and the "Bells," and many a gem beside of noble verse; who illustrated that power of the English tongue in prose composition not less logical than imaginative; and I forget the abuse, whether with or without foundation, that ignorance, prejudice or envy has heaped upon his memory. Unfortunate in the first biography following his death, where the author, with a temper difficult to understand, actually seemed to enjoy the depreciation of the poet's life, Edgar Allan Poe was seen by a malignant eye, and his story was told by an unkindly tongue ; and the efforts since made by friends to do him justice are slowly succeeding in demonstrating that there was in him an amount of good which, in all fairness, should be set off against that which we must regret while we attempt to palliate.

To Poe, there well may be applied the verse of one of the most gifted of our poetesses, addressed to a great name in a very different sphere :

> " The moss upon thy memory, no !
> Not while one note is rung
> Of those divine, immortal lays
> Milton and Shakspeare sung ;
> Not till the gloom of night ensbroud
> The Anglo-Saxon tongue."

REMARKS BY MR. NEILSON POE.

After Mr. Latrobe had concluded his remarks, Mr. Neilson Poe, Sr., a cousin of the poet, was introduced by Prof. Elliott, and spoke as follows :—

Among the persons who have assembled here to-day to witness these affecting and impressive ceremonies, are a number of the kindred, in nearer or remoter degrees, of the author to whom you are about to dedicate an enduring monument. It has seemed to them that they would be wanting both in sensibility and gratitude, if they suffered the occasion to pass without some acknowledgment of their special obligations to the ladies and gentlemen by whose zeal and liberality this memorial has been erected. It is impossible that they, of all the world, can be indifferent to the constantly increasing fame of one whose ancestors were also their ancestors, or that they can disguise their pride and gratification in realising that the faults and foibles of their kinsman which malevolence and envy had invented or exaggerated, have, under more impartial and deliberate examination, come to be judged with more of charity and more of justice. The large audience here to-day, the interest which the press and the public throughout the country have evinced in these ceremonies, the multiplication of editions of his works on both sides of the Atlantic, and in most of the Continental tongues, and the concurring voice of scholars and reviewers everywhere, all prove beyond dispute that his fame is not either local or ephemeral, and that, in the language of the most renowned of critics, he is not to be regarded as a transitory meteor of the lower sky, shedding a waning or a borrowed lustre, but rather as a star of the upper firmament, destined to shine with a fixed and unalterable glory.

On behalf, therefore, of all who bear his name or share his blood, I return their profound thanks, and, in their name, declare their complete satisfaction with the results of the labors of the generous and enthusiastic authors of this tribute to his memory, and with the energy, judgment and good taste which have marked all their proceedings.

Those present then repaired to Westminster Churchyard, where all that is mortal of Poe reposes. The remains have been removed from their first resting-place, in an obscure part of the lot, to the corner of Fayette and Greene streets, where the monument now covering the grave can be seen from Fayette street.

While the Philharmonic Society rendered the dirge "Sleep and Rest," by Barnby, the Committee on the Memorial and others gathered around the monument. The dirge is an adaptation of Tennyson's "Sweet and Low," by Mrs. Eleanor Fullerton, of this city. Prof. Elliott and Miss Rice removed the muslin in which the memorial was veiled while the dirge was being sung, and the memorial was then for the first time presented to the gaze of the public. The monument was crowned with a wreath composed of ivy, and another of lilies and evergreens. After the dirge, Mr. William F. Gill, of Boston, recited Poe's poem, "Annabel Lee," and Mrs. Dillehunt, a former school-teacher, selections from "The Bells." This concluded the exercises, and the throng which had collected in the graveyard came forward to view the monument.

During the exercises a large throng was gathered in the vicinity of Fayette and Greene streets, unable to gain admission to the Female High School or the churchyard.

THE MONUMENT.

The monument is of the pedestal or cippus form, eight feet high; the surbase is of Woodstock granite, six feet square and one foot thick; the rest being of fine white veined Italian marble. The pedestal has an Attic base three feet ten inches square; the die-block is a cube three feet square and three feet two inches high, relieved on each face by a square projecting and polished panel, the upper angles of which are broken and filled with a carved rosette. On the front panel is the bas-relief bust of the poet, modelled by Frederick Volck from a photograph, and executed in the finest statuary marble. On the opposite panel is inscribed the dates of the poet's birth and death. On the Attic base below the front panel is the name of EDGAR ALLAN POE, in large raised letters. The die-block is crowned by a bold and graceful frieze and cornice four feet square, broken on each face in the centre by the segment of a circle. The frieze is ornamented at the angles by richly-carved acanthus leaves, and in the circled centres by a lyre crowned with laurel. The whole is capped by a blocking three feet square, cut to a low pyramidal form. The effect of the whole admirably carries out the design of the architect, which was to produce "something simple, chaste, and dignified, to strike more by graceful outlines and proportions, than by crowding with unmeaning ornament."

A pleasing feature of the ceremonies was the placing upon the monument of a large wreath of flowers, made up principally of camellias, lilies and tea-roses. Together with this was deposited a floral tribute in the shape of a raven, made from black immortelles. The large petals of the lilies suggested the "Bells" immortalised by Poe's genius, the significance of the other emblem being obvious. These were tributes from the company at Ford's Grand Opera House, Mrs. Germon being mainly instrumental in getting them up. Poe's mother had been an actress at Holliday Street Theatre, which fact had been preserved in the traditions of the stage and had something to do with inspiring this tribute.

Letters

from

Poets and Authors.

Feb 18ᵗʰ/76

Madam

How can so strange & fine
a genius & so sad a life be expressed
& compressed in one ⬛ line —
would it not be best to say
of Poe in a reverential spirit
simply Requiescat in Pace

A Tennyson

Nov. 9th 1875

Dear Madam,

I have heard with much pleasure
of the memorial at length raised to
your illustrious fellow-citizen. The genius
of Edgar Poe has won on this side of
the Atlantic such wide & warm recogni-
-tion that the sympathy which I cannot
hope fitly or fully to express in adequate
words is undoubtedly shared at this
moment by hundreds as far as the
news may have spread throughout
not England only but France as well;
where as I need not remind you the
most beautiful & durable of monuments

has been reared to the genius of Poe
by the laborious devotion of a genius
equal & akin to his own: nature
the admirable translation of
his prose works by a fellow-poet
whom also we have now to lament
before his time is even now being
perfected by a careful & exquisite
version of his poems, with illustration
full of the notable & tragic force
of fancy which impelled & moulded
the original song; a double

homage due to the loyal & loving co-
-operation of one of the most remarkable
younger poets & one of the most
powerful leading painters in France
– M. Mallarmé & M. Manet.

It is not for me to offer any
tribute here to the fame of
your great countryman, or dilate
with superfluous & intrusive
admiration on the special quality
of his sharp & delicate genius, so
sure of aim & faultless of touch in
all the better & finer parts of

work he has left us; I would only, in conveying to the members of the Poe Memorial Committee my sincere acknowledgment of the honour they have done me in recalling my name on such an occasion, take leave to express my firm conviction that widely as the fame of Poe has already spread & deeply as it is already rooted in Europe it is even now growing wider & striking deeper as time advances; the surest presage that time, the eternal enemy of small & shallow reputations, will prove in this case also the constant & trusty friend & keeper of a true poet's full-grown fame.

I remain (Dear Madam) Yours very truly
A. C. Swinburne

Sara S. Rice
            dear friend,

The extraordinary genius
of Edgar Poe is now
acknowledged the world
over, and the proffered
tribute to his memory
indicates a full appre-
ciation of his rare
intellectual gifts on
the part of the city of
his birth, as a matter
of principle. I do not
favor ostentatious

monuments for the dead, but sometimes it seems the only way to express the appreciation which circumstances in some measure may have denied to the living man.

I am not able to be present at the inauguration of the monument. Pray express my thanks to the ladies & gentlemen for whom thy letter speaks, for the invitation acknowledging the kind terms in which thy invitation was conveyed on thy part. I am very truly thy friend

John G. Whittier

Dear Madam.

I comply with your request so far as to send you the draught of an epitaph for the monument to Edgar A. Poe; which you will adopt, or modify, or change, or reject wholly, as may please you and those who are concerned in the project to which you refer. You do not say whether it (the monument) is to be erected over his grave. If it is to be so, the addition of the date of his birth and that of his death, which I have left partly in blank, would be necessary.

I am Madam,
faithfully yours,
W. C. Bryant.

Prof. S. S. Rice.

To Edgar Allan Poe.
Author of the Raven
and other poems,
(And various works of Fiction,
distinguished alike
for originality in the Conception,
skill in word=painting,
and power over the mind of the reader,
The public school teachers
of Baltimore,
admirers of his genius,
have erected this monument.

He was born January — 1811,
and died — — 18⁴⁹.

Coombe. Apr. 20.
1875.

Dear Madam,

The only lines of Mr.
Poe that I now recall
as in any way appro-
priate to the purpose
you mention, are from
a poem entitled "For

Annie". They are

"The fever called Living
Is conquered at last."

But I dare say you
will be able to find
something better.
  In great haste.
    Yours truly
Henry W. Longfellow.

Dear Miss Rice,

In answer to your kind invitation I regret that I cannot say that I hope to be present at the ceremony of placing a monument over the grave of your poet. Your city has already honored valor and patriotism by the erection of stately columns. Republics are said to be ungrateful, perhaps because they have short memories, forgetting wrongs as quickly as benefits, but your city has shown that it can remember and has taught us all the lesson of gratitude.

No one, surely, needs a mausoleum less than the poet.

His monument shall be his gentle verse
Which eyes not yet created shall o'er read,
And tongues to be his being shall rehearse
When all the breathers of this world are dead.

Yet we would not leave him without a stone to mark the spot where the hand that waked to ecstasy the living lyre were laid in the dust. He who can confer

an immortality which will outlast
bronze and granite deserves this poor
tribute, not for his sake so much as can
the hearts of all who reverence the
inspiration of genius, who can look tenderly
upon the infirmities too often attending it,
who can feel for its misfortunes will sympathise with you as you gather around
the resting-place of all that was mortal
of Edgar Allan Poe and raise the stone
inscribed with one of the few names which
will outlive the graven record meant to
perpetuate its remembrance.

Believe me
Very truly yours
O. W. Holmes.

FROM RICHARD HENGIST HORNE.

(Author of " Orion," " Cosmo de' Medici," &c.)

LONDON, *April* 8, 1876.

To do adequate justice to a genius so original and so varied as that of Edgar Allan Poe, would require far more space than can be allotted to a mere letter. A few leading features only can be sketched as indicated. This is the more to be regretted, because of the extraordinary pains he bestowed in considering, designing, and elaborating with the highest and most minute finishing, almost every subject he adopted. No cunning barrister preparing an important brief; no great actor studying a new part; no machinist brooding over the invention of an engine, or a change subversive of the old machinery; no analytic chemist seeking to establish the fact of a murder by the discovery and proof of blood or poison in some unexpected substance; no Dutch painter working for months on the minute finish of all sorts of details in the background as well as foreground of his picture,—ever took more pains than did Edgar Allan Poe in the production of most of his principal works. The more impossible his story, the more perseveringly, learnedly, patiently, and plausibly he laboured to prove the facts as he saw them. And, unless you throw the book down, he always succeeds. If you read on steadily, you must go with him. You must believe in his mesmerism, his mummy, and his more than "detective" acumen in tracing a horrible murder to the "escaped convict" of a menagerie; you are with him in the unswamped, frantic little boat, whirling round the interior of the maelstrom; and you most certainly make a voyage with Hans Pfaall to the moon, admiring all his scientific previsions and manœuvres, and delighted with all the somewhat alarming wonders through which he navigates you. Since the voyage of Mr. Lemuel Gulliver to the island of Laputa, there has been nothing of this class comparable to the reasoned-out story, or lunatic "log"— for it is both — of Hans Pfaall.

Not that the story is any imitation, or bears anything beyond an aërial resemblance to the wonderful narrative of Dean Swift. Among all literary man, Poe stands very much alone, and should be judged by his own standard. It will be well if we tried to do this in all cases of original genius. If it be true that we judge of all things by comparison, still there is, no doubt, a stupid and slavish degree to which this is often carried. In the power of describing imaginary, and even miraculous scenes, actions and events, Poe possesses a kind of similarity to Swift, and also to some of the writers in the "Arabian Nights," and among the Hebrews, ancient Persians, and other Oriental fabulists; but while Poe's narratives excite an equally rivetting interest and apprehension, they are not, for the most part, beautiful or poetical, though we must admit several marked exceptions of somewhat depressing loveliness and melancholy fascination. We have heard people say that they wished they had never read some of the stories, so painfully penetrating had been the influence. Let no one endeavour to imitate Edgar Allan Poe. Without his genius and acquirements, such subjects would be intolerable, and the copyist would be discovered and denounced in an instant. The great majority of the fashionable novels of the day are no better than doll-houses by the side of his brain-haunted structures.

During a certain period of Poe's troubled circumstances, he wrote to me, I being then in London, and inclosed a manuscript, saying that he had singled me out, though personally a stranger, to ask the friendly service of handing a certain story to the editor of one of the magazines, with a view, of course, to some remittance. Without waiting to read the story, I replied at once that I considered his application to me a great compliment, and that I would certainly do the best I could in the business. But when I read the sto. my heart of hope sank within me: it was "The Spectacles." I tried several magazines. Not an editor would touch it. In vain I represented the remarkable tact with which the old lady, under the very trying task she had set herself, did, nevertheless, maintain her female delicacy and dignity. I met with nothing beyond a deaf ear, an uplifted eyebrow, or the ejaculations of a gentleman pretending to feel quite shocked. It may be that false modesty, and social, as well as religious, hypocrisy, are the concomitant and counterpart of our present equivocal state of civilisation; but if I were not an Englishman, it is more than probable I should say that those qualities were more glaringly conspicuous in England than in any other country.

With regard to the poems of Edgar Allan Poe, they have been in certain instances mistaken by admirers in many parts of the world,— not for any rare qualities they really possess, but for something they have not. General readers of poetry, especially youthful readers, have been led away—we will not call it "led astray"—by his weird music. Also by the studied artifice of his selection, or coinage, of liquid and sonorous sounds and words, such as (to spell them phonetically) *ullaleume—annabellee—ells* (in the "Bells") *ōre*, in "The Raven," which abounds in that long-drawn tone. It is too obviously artificial, and seems to supersede inspiration. The poet himself appears to have taken a strange pleasure in describing the almost mechanical plan and execution of the poem for which he is most celebrated. A critic has suggested that this statement was probably an afterthought. Possibly it was one of Poe's analytic freaks; and yet, when we see clearly the forethought he must have devoted to the working-out of his stories, I regret to say that I more than half believe his statement about the very unpoetical hatching of his Raven. "Heresy and schism!" As for the charming melody, liquid flow, and luring pathos of some of his lyrics, there can be no question of the success of the versification, by whatever means produced. Now and then the poems look deep, but that is often owing to their pellucid clearness, and there is not very much at the bottom. It is in the unique invention, and mastery of execution in his prose tales, that the genius of Poe most potently displays itself. There is nothing like them in the English, or any other language.

How I rejoiced when I read the recent refutation of the gross slanders and envenomed detractions with which the name and fame of Edgar Allan Poe had been for so many years environed! How I clapped my hands when I saw Mr. Ingram dig out the old vipers and burn the hornets' nests! But my rejoicing was chiefly on account of the rectification of the world's opinion : as for my own, I had never believed much beyond the accusations of intemperance; and as to the worst of the rest, I had always felt—*in the absence of Poe's own defence*—that life, especially in one like him, was "a mingled yarn," and that certain natures seldom have fair play.

While congratulating all Poe's countrymen who have raised a monument to his memory, I am reminded that at this very time there is a movement (originated in Rome) for getting a bust of Keats placed in Westminster Abbey. How Keats was treated while living, we know too well; and how little valued was Poe, we also know. Will these things ever warn the world of such of its living benefactors as may be in like manner neglected?

RICHARD HENGIST HORNE.

FROM GEORGE W. CHILDS.

. . . . . There is a mournful satisfaction even in this late tribute to one whose rare genius and sensitive nature were accompanied by so many unhappy experiences of life. Poor Poe! his working-day world was more than full of sorrows,— and he seems to have been happy only in his visions outside of real life, or in his dream of a world beyond that in which we all live.

What is now being done by affectionate friends, and by those who feel that injustice has been done to his memory, may prove to be the starting-point of a changed and juster view of his life and character. Although it is far too late to be of service to him, it is not too late to be of benefit to ourselves and others. Those of us who may have felt disposed to censure him, can read with profit the following lines from his "Tamerlane," and especially the last couplet:—

—"I firmly do believe —
I know — for Death who comes for me
From regions of the blest afar,
Where there is nothing to deceive,
Hath left his iron gate ajar;
And *rays of truth you can not see*
Are flashing through eternity."

GEORGE W. CHILDS.

FROM W. C. BRYANT.

I comply with your request so far as to send you the draught of an epitaph for the monument to Edgar A. Poe.

W. C. BRYANT.

To
EDGAR ALLAN POE,
Author of the Raven
and other poems,
and of various works of Fiction
distinguished alike
for originality in the conception,
skill in word-painting,
and power over the mind of the reader,
THE PUBLIC SCHOOL TEACHERS
of
Baltimore,
admirers of his genius,
have erected this monument.

FROM S. D. LEWIS.

BROOKLYN, N. Y., *Oct.* 11, 1875.

Allow me, a personal friend and warm admirer of both the genius and the personal worth of our lamented friend, to say to you and to the Association a few words.

I have resided and practised my profession of the law in Brooklyn for about thirty years. Shortly after I moved here, in 1845, Mr. Poe and I became personal friends. His last residence, and where I visited him oftenest, was in a beautifully secluded cottage at Fordham, fourteen miles above New York. It was there that I often saw his dear wife during her last illness, and attended her funeral. It was from there that he and his "dear Muddie" (Mrs. Clemm) often visited me at my house, frequently, and at my urgent solicitation, remaining many days. When he finally departed on his last trip south, the kissing and handshaking were at my front-door. He was hopeful; we were sad: and tears gushed in torrents as he kissed his "dear Muddie" and my wife, "good-bye." Alas, it proved, as Mrs. Clemm feared, a final adieu.

A few months afterwards, on receipt of the sad news of his death, I offered Mrs. Clemm a home in my family, where she resided until 1858, when she removed to Baltimore to lay her ashes by the side of her "darling Eddie." I hold many of her precious, loving, grateful letters to me from there, up to a few days before her death.

And now as to Mr. Poe. He was one of the most affectionate, kind-hearted men I ever knew. I never witnessed so much tender affection and devoted love as existed in that family of three persons. His dear Virginia, after her death, was his "lost Lenore." I have spent weeks in the closest intimacy with Mr. Poe, and I never saw him drink a drop of liquor, wine or beer, in my life; and never saw him under the slightest influence of any stimulants whatever. He was, in truth, a most abstemious and exemplary man. But I learned from Mrs. Clemm that if, on the importunity of a convivial friend, he took a single glass, even of wine, it suddenly flashed through his nervous system and excitable brain; and that he was no longer himself or responsible for his acts. His biographers have not done his virtues or his genius justice; and to produce a startling effect by contrast, have magnified his errors and attributed to him faults which he never had.

He was always in my presence the polished gentleman, the profound scholar, the true critic, and the inspired oracular poet—dreamy and spiritual, lofty, but sad. His memory is green and fresh in many admiring and loving hearts; and your work of erecting a monument over his grave, if it adds nothing to his fame, reflects honor on you and your association, and upon all who sympathise or assist in your noble work.

I am proud to assure you, and the association through you, that his many friends are grateful and thank you.

> "What recks he of their plaudits now?
> He never deemed them worth his care;
> And death has twined about his brow
> The wreath he was too proud to wear."

S. D. LEWIS.

FROM MRS. MARGARET J. PRESTON.

LEXINGTON, VIRGINIA, *Oct. 8th.*

I thank you for the good opinion which led you to propose the writing of a poem on my part, for the prospective inauguration of the Poe memorial. While it is not in my power to comply with the flattering request, or to be present at the ceremonial, I tender to the Committee my thanks, nevertheless, for the honor thus conferred on me. There would seem to be a slight appropriateness in the proposal made to *me*, inasmuch as my husband (Col. Preston, of the Virginia Military College) was a boyish friend of Poe's, when they went to school together in Richmond, who used to sit on the same bench with him, and together with him pore over the same pages of Horace. To him, as his earliest literary critic,— a boy of fourteen — Poe was accustomed to bring his first verses. Even then, youth as he was, he was distinguished by many of the characteristics which marked his after life.

MARGARET J. PRESTON.

FROM JOHN GODFREY SAXE.

BROOKLYN, N. Y., Oct. 10, 1875.

I avail myself of your friendly note to express my interest in the event and my admiration of the noble-hearted men and women of Baltimore, who, by the erection of a beautiful and appropriate monument to the memory of Edgar A. Poe, perform a patriotic office which was primarily and peculiarly the duty, as it should have been the pride, of the American *Literati* toward one whose original genius has done so much to adorn and distinguish American literature.

JOHN GODFREY SAXE.

FROM MRS. SARAH HELEN WHITMAN.

PROVIDENCE, Nov. 5, 1875.

I need not say to you that the generous efforts of the Association in whose behalf you write, have called forth my warmest sympathy and most grateful appreciation.

The work so long delayed has been consummated at the *right time*, and through the most congenial and appropriate agencies.

SARAH HELEN WHITMAN.

FROM JOHN NEAL.

PORTLAND, ME., *Nov.* 3, 1875.

You have brought to my recollection, as from their graves, many of my dear old friends; and I assure you that Baltimore is my beloved city, and that nothing would gratify me more than to find myself there with the wishing-cap of Fortunatus at my elbow, so that I might find myself here again in the twinkling of an eye, if I suddenly wanted.

Edgar A. Poe was a wonderful man, and he has never had justice done him. Most happy should I be, if in my power, to witness the ceremony of the inauguration of his monument; for after all the abominable calumnies that have been circulated against him, both abroad and at home, he stands higher to-day in the estimation of kindred poets than he ever did while on earth.

He says in one of his letters that I gave him the first push in his upward career, and for that reason was bound to keep him moving.

JOHN NEAL.

FROM JOHN H. INGRAM.

LONDON, ENGLAND, *16th November*, 1875.

I thank you and your Committee for the honor they do me in inviting any expression of my opinion with respect to the object of their labours, but during the last few years my views respecting Edgar Allan Poe have been so frequently brought before the public that I fear a repetition of them upon the present occasion is scarcely likely to prove interesting. I have little faith in "heaps of stones" as memorials of the great, but must confess that a public expression of admiration for an illustrious son whose memory has been so long overclouded by unmerited obloquy does seem fitting on the part of America.

JOHN H. INGRAM.

FROM THOMAS BAILEY ALDRICH.

BOSTON, MASSACHUSETTS, *Oct.* 10, 1875.

Your desire to honor Poe's genius is in the heart of every man of letters, though perhaps no American author stands so little in need of a monument to perpetuate his memory as the author of "The Raven." His imperishable fame is in all lands.

THOMAS BAILEY ALDRICH.

FROM PROF. JAMES WOOD DAVIDSON.

WASHINGTON, D. C., *23rd Nov.*, 1875.

My admiration of Poe's genius is as old as my knowledge of it; and I was roused to indignation in his behalf by the persistent and palpably malignant efforts to damn him with some drops of faint praise, and some oceans of strong abuse.

The tide has turned. The almost universal favour that Mr. Ingram's *Memoir* — which demolishes Mr. Griswold's — and complete edition of his *Works*, have met with in England especially, but also in America, clearly indicates the turn. And your monument speaks the same gratifying truth. France and Germany also have said the same thing.

JAMES WOOD DAVIDSON.

FROM PROF. JOHN DIMITRY.

BARRANQUILLA, U. S. OF COLOMBIA, S. A.,
Dec. 24, 1875.

Permit me to transmit a memorial inscription in honor of the great writer whose monument has already been — or is soon to be — through your public-spirited efforts, reared and dedicated in Baltimore.

I am a sincere admirer of Edgar A. Poe. I have long considered him at once the greatest original genius our country has produced; and, beyond all doubt, the greatest genius born, with an English-speaking tongue, in the nineteenth century.

JOHN DIMITRY.

To
EDGAR ALLAN POE.
Who, in his Poetry, struck but few Notes,
Yet these, now the tenderest, now the saddest,
That translate human Passions
Into melodious Words,
And so fix them forever;
Who, in his Prose, Master of the Passions and of Style,
Wielding, with equal Skill,
The Brand of Terror and the Wand of Humor,
At his Will, thrilled men to Horror, or stirred them to
Laughter,
In whose Tales
Whether they be sombre, or wild unto grotesqueness,
Religion can find no Offence, Virtue no Wrong,
Nor Innocence take Alarm;
And who, passing a Life chequered enough to serve for Warning,
Censure railing with loud Voice, while Praise came but in Whispers,
Has, through a Genius lifted victoriously above Detraction,
Happily, made sure of
Posterity;
THIS MONUMENT,
A Tribute to his Memory by Admiring Townsmen,
Has been erected
In his Native City.

FROM G. HERBERT SASS ("BARTON GREY.")

CHARLESTON, S. C., *March* 30, 1876.

I embrace gladly the opportunity afforded me of expressing my satisfaction at the Memorial you are now preparing to Edgar

Allan Poe. It was time that the South should do something to prove her appreciation of the most exquisite and subtle genius she has produced. Of course Poe's best monument is his own immortal verse; and the tardy justice the world is now doing him is but the inevitable result of the ample vindication of Time. But his fellow-countrymen, to whom his fame is dear, and still more his fellow-craftsmen, who owe him so large a debt, must gratefully recognise the unselfish labours of those who have helped to make the memory of the man as clear as must always be the renown of the poet.

I can not help thinking that the final verdict of criticism must confirm the popular feeling, and that Poe will be acknowledged by posterity as an artist almost peerless in his own sphere, however limited that sphere may be adjudged to be.

G. HERBERT SASS.

Poetic Tributes.

— ✦ —

LE TOMBEAU D'EDGAR POE.

SONNET.

Tel qu'en lui-même enfin l'éternité le change,
Le poëte suscite avec un hymne nu
Son siècle épouvanté de n'avoir pas connu
Que la mort s'exaltait dans cette voix étrange :

Mais, comme un vil tressant d'hydre, oyant jadis l'ange
Donner un sens plus pur aux mots de la tribu,
Tous pensèrent entre eux le sortilège bu
Chez le flot sans honneur de quelque noir mélange.

Du sol et de l'éther hostiles, ô grief !
Si mon idée avec ne sculpte un bas-relief
Dont la tombe de Poe eblouissante s'orne,

Sombre bloc à jamais chu d'un désastre obscur,
Que ce granit du moins montre à jamais sa borne
Aux vieux vols de blasphème epars dans le futur.

STÉPHANE MALLARMÉ.

POE.

Two mighty spirits dwelt in him:
One, a wild demon, weird and dim,
The darkness of whose ebon wings
Did shroud unutterable things:
One, a fair angel, in the skies
Of whose serene, unshadowed eyes
Were seen the lights of Paradise.

To these, in turn, he gave the whole
Vast empire of his brooding soul;
Now, filled with strains of heavenly swell,
Now, thrilled with awful tones of hell:
Wide were his being's strange extremes,
'Twixt nether glooms, and Eden gleams
Of tender, or majestic dreams.

But sapped by want, and riven by wrong,
His heart-chords took life's minor song,
Till rhythms of anguish only passed
Athwart their tortured strength, at last:
The angel fled with sigh and moan;
The demon spurned his vacant throne,
And ruled those dark domains alone.

Then, to the poet's brain there came
Nought but fierce visions, breathing flame;
Spectres of gibbering horror pale,
All creatures of the house of bale:
His fate remorseless urged him o'er
Oceans that stretched without a shore,
Whose swart waves whispered " NEVERMORE ! "

Ever, that whisper wandered low,
Across life's weltering ebb and flow;
It touched at length — a sad refrain —
The sources of his deepest pain,
Set their dull currents rippling by
In concords far too sweet to die,
Wedding despair to harmony.

Henceforth, with pinions seldom furled,
His sombre "Raven" roams the world:
All stricken peoples pause to hear
The echo of his burden drear;
For ah! the deathless type is he
Of pangs we may not shun, nor flee,—
And grief's stern immortality.

PAUL H. HAYNE.

EDGAR A. POE.

He loved all shadowy spots, all seasons drear;
  All ways of darkness lured his ghastly whim;
  Strange fellowships he held with goblins grim,
At whose demoniac eyes he felt no fear.
On midnights through dense branches he would peer,
  To watch the pale ghoul feed by tombstones dim;
  The appalling forms of phantoms walked with him,
And murder breathed its red guilt in his ear.

By desolate paths of dream where fancy's owl
  Sent long lugubrious hoots through sombre air,
Amid thought's gloomiest caves he went to prowl
  And met delirium in her awful lair,
And mingled with cold shapes that writhe or scowl —
  Serpents of horror, black bats of despair.

EDGAR FAWCETT.

www.ingramcontent.com/pod-product-compliance
Lightning Source LLC
Chambersburg PA
CBHW060246030726
47493CB00025B/2702